A PROMISE FOR TOMORROW

A Promise for Tomorrow

Sheila Spencer-Smith

THORNDIKE
CHIVERS

This Large Print edition is published by Thorndike Press, Waterville, Maine, USA and by BBC Audiobooks Ltd, Bath, England.
Thorndike Press, a part of Gale, Cengage Learning.
Copyright © Sheila Spencer-Smith, 2005.
The moral right of the author has been asserted.

LIBRARY OF CONGRESS CATALOGING-IN-PUBLICATION DATA

Spencer-Smith, Sheila.
  A promise for tomorrow / by Sheila Spencer-Smith.
    p. cm. — (Thorndike Press large print candlelight)
  ISBN-13: 978-1-4104-0464-0 (hardcover : alk. paper)
  ISBN-10: 1-4104-0464-1 (hardcover : alk. paper)
  1. Large type books. I. Title.
  PR6069.P487P76 2008
  823'.914—dc22   2007044593

BRITISH LIBRARY CATALOGUING-IN-PUBLICATION DATA AVAILABLE
Published in 2008 in the U.S. by arrangement with Dorian Literary Agency.
Published in 2008 in the U.K. by arrangement with the author.
U.K. Hardcover: 978 1 405 64360 3 (Chivers Large Print)
U.K. Softcover: 978 1 405 64361 0 (Camden Large Print)

Printed in the United States of America
1 2 3 4 5 6 7 12 11 10 09 08

A Promise for Tomorrow

CHAPTER ONE

"Here we come, camera," Melissa said, shaking back her mane of unruly fair hair as she unlocked the door of her Fiesta and slid inside. "A challenge, that's what we've got, you and I, and let's not forget it."

She patted her new digital camera on the passenger seat beside her. Firbright Photographers had been generous with their leaving present. Having worked as their receptionist for just under a year, she hadn't expected anything like this when she left to get married and move away. She knew her eyes had shone with happiness as she made her farewells and slipped away from the building, full of confidence that her future was mapped out exactly the way she wanted it.

How wrong she had been.

With a sigh Melissa put the car into gear, released the handbrake and set off across the heath. The mass of dark clouds above her gave a sombre look to the flat landscape though ahead rounded green hills beckoned.

What was she doing in this strange place far from friends and family? How different to have started out on a new life here as planned with Damien by her side to share in the fresh experiences as they settled down to married life together.

But she was here on her own. She had to stick to the decision she had made now her fiancé had decided that they had no future together, and instead had gone abroad. In any case someone else had taken over her job as receptionist back home. She had nowhere to live either because a new flatmate had moved in as soon as she left to go home, a week before what should have been her wedding day.

But worst of all Damien was no longer on the scene.

Melissa shuddered and gripped the steering wheel. At first when he telephoned her to break the terrible news there had been a merciful blur, but then in the days that followed a vague and shamed feeling swept over her while her distracted parents dealt with everything that had to be done.

They had been simply brilliant and she didn't know what she would have done without them. But it wouldn't do for her to

8

stay there and brood, reminded all the time of what she had lost. Supportive as always, they had backed her decision to take up the new job on the Dorset coast because it was miles away in a new part of the country.

Through the open car window the air was bracing and smelt faintly of peat. Melissa took a deep breath and let it out slowly. She must think of what was ahead and mentally dump the past weeks into oblivion. It was what she had told herself so many times. But how could she banish Damien from her mind so easily?

For a second, yesterday evening, she had thought she glimpsed his fair head among the other guests in the dining-room of the guesthouse where she had booked in for the night. She discovered her mistake with a jerk of disappointment. Then she pushed back her chair and escaped into the hall. Hearing someone approach, she pretended interest in the row of information leaflets laid out in neat piles on the table against the wall.

"Are you all right, dear?" the landlady asked in concern.

Melissa picked up one of the leaflets and nodded. Fighting back the tears, she stared down at the paper in her hand. Then, gaining control, she looked up at the photographs of the castle adorning the walls. Each was taken from a different angle but all were impressive.

"Quite a landmark," the landlady said. "You'll be passing there tomorrow on your way to Trailover. It's worth a stop, my dear, if you've got the time."

Melissa nodded again and tried to smile. To please her she started to read the information in the leaflet as if she was merely on holiday instead of on the way to start a new job as personal assistant to the owner of Trailover House Hotel because, unlike Damien who immediately resigned from his new job in this area, she wasn't prepared to let the owner down. The words on the page danced before her eyes but she persevered even after the landlady had returned to her other guests.

Now Melissa's first view of the castle gave her an unexpected jolt though she had so recently seen its photograph. One man going out through a small doorway on water-duty during the siege in the Civil War had betrayed the castle in the end.

Parking her car on the edge of the village, she got out and walked closer. Looking up at the keep was amazing. She raised her camera to her eyes, clicked and then lowered it again.

She got back into the car and drove the few remaining miles up the narrow lane to the top of a hill and then down the steep winding lane that was signposted to Trailover House. Two men were erecting a large signboard nearby. The words Trailover House Hotel were emblazoned on it in gold paint. Arrangements were obviously completed for the changeover from a private dwelling to a hotel and that was good.

A shiver of anticipation ran down her spine. The sea in the distance sparkled blue and silver now the sky had cleared. Suddenly she felt sure she had done the right thing in coming to work here even though she still needed to find somewhere to live.

"Melissa Brown? Hi, there. I've been expecting you. Come on in."

"Not Brown," Melissa said. "Feilden. But yes, I'm Melissa."

She smiled at the small person who stood stoutly in the doorway of Trailover House looking as if she was ready to repel an invading army. Her straggly brown hair framed a small pinched face that suddenly broke into a charming smile and made her look years younger.

"I'm Poppy Dean." She shot her hand out and took Melissa's in a firm grip. "Housekeeper."

"Hi, Poppy."

"By heck, so you've changed your name."

"The opposite," Melissa said. "I kept my maiden name. I didn't get married after all."

At once the housekeeper's expression changed to one of sympathy but she said nothing. Instead she indicated that Melissa should follow her inside. "A cup of tea's what you need," she said briskly. "The kettle's on the boil. Nic, the boss, isn't expected back till twelve."

The red-carpeted hall looked welcoming. In the alcove beneath the stairs the mahogany table shone and there was the scent of beeswax on the air.

"I've just finished in here," Poppy said, looking round critically. "Aye, it's a good time for you to arrive. Come through to the kitchen."

The kettle on the Aga was bubbling gently. Poppy made tea and placed the teapot on a tray that stood ready on one side. She carried it across to the table in the middle of the room. Melissa seated herself opposite her and accepted a biscuit from the heaped plate Poppy offered.

"So," said Poppy when she had dealt with the pouring out and handed a mug of tea to Melissa. "You're the new PA. I didn't think much of the last one. She couldn't stand the place and cleared off after a couple of weeks. Said the area was too creepy. The boss were mad I can tell you. I'm glad you won't do the same."

"How can you be sure of that?"

"Well, you came, didn't you? You didn't opt out when it suited. It couldn't have been easy."

"I didn't want to let Mr Haldane down."

"Nic. He likes to be called Nic. I'm right glad you're here."

Melissa smiled at the warm Yorkshire tones in Poppy's voice. "You sound far from home too, Poppy."

"Aye. An adventurer, that's me. I like to go all over the place and not settle for long." Poppy drank her tea scalding hot and then leapt up to refill the kettle. "I'll move on from here in a month or two I shouldn't wonder." She placed the kettle on the Aga and sat down again. "Olivia couldn't be better pleased."

"Olivia?"

"Trouble, that one. Had it in for me from the first. Thought I was after Nic, I suppose." Poppy leaned back in her chair and laughed derisively.

Looking at her, Melissa could see that the kindness and good humour in her small face gave her a beauty all her own. She had the

13

feeling that no-one would get the better of Poppy Dean and felt all the better for knowing that.

"As if I'd chase another woman's man," Poppy said.

She looked stoutly independent in her sensible dark jersey and jeans. Melissa found it hard to imagine her chasing the tall elegant-looking Nic Haldane, desperate for a bit of romance. When Melissa had met him in Leeds when she interviewed for the job he had seemed pleasant but unapproachable.

"Who's Olivia?" she asked.

Poppy leaned forward, grabbed the teapot and poured a streaming flow of liquid into her empty mug. "The lady of the manor."

Bemused, Melissa sipped her tea thoughtfully. Nic Haldane had made it plain he wasn't married. He had seemed to like the fact that when she took up her post here as his personal assistant she would be wearing a wedding ring on her finger.

Poppy leapt up again to push the kettle slightly off the heat source. "You'll know that they converted Trailover House into a hotel last winter? Nic met the gorgeous Olivia on some skiing holiday, more's the pity. Now she thinks she owns the place."

"I see."

"Calls herself his business partner. She comes and goes though. Got her own place up in London and wants to live there permanently. I don't know why she got herself hooked up with Nic. No way is he going to sell up and move on."

Melissa wondered how she could be so certain, but didn't want to ask. It wasn't her place to discuss her employer's private life.

"So are you still going to be living in Stanford?" Poppy asked, coming to sit down again. "That was the address you gave, wasn't it?"

"Not any more." Damien had cancelled their flat there when he decided not to take up his new job but go abroad instead. "I booked in at a guesthouse in Trant Magna last night so I could get here early. It's OK for the next few nights too, but then they're booked up. I need to find somewhere cheaper in the long term, if I can."

"Here of course," Poppy said. "There's loads of room in a place this size. You'll be on the spot for work and not have to travel. We're isolated here and there's nowhere nearby so you've not got much choice. The last PA had her own accommodation here. Pick up your things, Melissa. There's a room ready."

"Are you sure that's all right? Won't Mr

Haldane, Nic, object?"

"Why should her? No problem. He'll be happy you're suited. And Olivia can take a running jump."

Melissa smiled at Poppy's ferocious expression. She finished her tea and stood up. "Thanks, Poppy. That was great."

The room Poppy had ready for Melissa was on the second floor at the back.

"What a view!" Melissa said as she went in. From here she could look out across a stretch of heathland to green hills silhouetted against the faint sky. No trees broke up the bare expanse but there were strange little structures at intervals and a red flag here and there. She knew that Trailover House was close to a wide area used as a firing range and she had seen the notices to keep out when the red flags were flying.

"This is far too grand for me," she said. "Are you sure you should put me here?"

"I'm the housekeeper, aren't I?" Poppy said. "What I say goes."

"But Poppy, look at the size of it. One small room would do me. And I couldn't afford to pay for anything like this."

"Who said anything about paying?" Poppy said airily.

Melissa was unconvinced. She resolved not to unpack her suitcases until she had asked about her accommodation with her new boss. He might have entirely different ideas. He had checked at the interview that she and her prospective new husband wished to live in their own place and that she would commute each day. He wouldn't be expecting this.

Melissa moved towards the door. "I'll unpack later, Poppy. How about showing me round so I get a feel for the place? I know more or less what's expected of me but I'd like to see everything for myself."

"So you'll likely be a sort of dogsbody," Poppy said, her head a little on one side.

Melissa smiled. "That's me." It had sounded like it when Nic Haldane tried to explain to her what her duties would be. They were mainly overseeing that all was going well with all aspects of the hotel business and taking charge when he was away.

As housekeeper, Poppy had a couple of people coming in by car two mornings a week to help her and there was Ted the gardener who did odd jobs too and looked after everything outside. But so much of her own job as Nic's personal assistant would be played by ear. She was looking forward to getting to grips with it.

"I'll show you Nic's office first," Poppy said. "He said to show you. You've got a small one next to it with a connecting door."

Melissa liked the large room with the computer and all the accessories on the wide desk. Everything in the room was neat and functional as if whoever worked here had a tidy mind.

The rest of the layout downstairs impressed her. The large and rambling house had been well converted. Two sunny reception rooms at the front had pleasant views towards the sea that was a shiny line on the horizon. One of them had a large terrace area outside the french windows on which someone had arranged tables and chairs invitingly.

The dining-room was suitably large too and close to the kitchen, and in both of them sunshine flooded in. Melissa followed Poppy from room to room listening to her as she said that they could take thirty guests maximum, and already the bookings for the coming season were pouring in.

"It's the Heritage Coast brings them," Poppy sniffed. "Archaeologists and the like, and people wanting to be on the newest thing. Not to mention the village of Trailover down below, even though there's little there to see. Ruins mostly."

Melissa knew about the deserted village that had been evacuated during the Second

World War for the area to be used as a firing range. The promise that the people would be able to return when peace came, was never kept. Much had been made of it lately in a TV programme. She was looking forward to visiting it on her first day off.

The sounds of a car being driven across the gravel drive interrupted Poppy's flow of words. "That'll be Nic now," she said.

CHAPTER TWO

Nic came in on a breeze of cool air. "Ah," he said on seeing Melissa. "So you're Melissa. Welcome to Trailover."

Melissa smiled and stood up. His handshake was warm and firm and she liked the way his sudden smile lit up features that might otherwise be described as stern. He placed his briefcase on the worktop and shrugged himself out of his jacket.

"Poppy's been looking after me," Melissa said.

He flashed a look of thanks at Poppy and nodded his head. "Well done. She's shown you the office, I take it, and explained about the first guests arriving tomorrow?"

"Aye, all that," Poppy said firmly. "And I've allotted her a room."

He raised his eyebrows. "A room?"

"To sleep in. On the first floor at the back, the mauve and white room with a view across to the ranges."

"Ah, yes, the ranges," he said. "The road down to the village is strictly out of bounds to guests and employees when the red flags are flying. We have to stress this most strongly for safety's sake, Melissa. Also, we'll be in deep trouble with the range warden if it's not enforced."

"She knows all that," Poppy said brusquely. "We all do."

"I needed accommodation after all," Melissa chipped in quickly. "I'm on my own now that my marriage didn't take place. But there's no problem, really. I can commute from Stanford if I can find something there."

The moment's silence seemed to her to drag on. Beside her, Poppy shifted her weight from one foot to the other.

"That won't be necessary," Nic said. "There's a room available on the top floor, only small, but I'm sure that won't bother you."

"Of course not," Melissa murmured with a glance at Poppy's reddening face. Thank goodness she hadn't unpacked her things and stowed them in the vast wardrobes of the room Poppy had shown her.

"I'll see you later," Nic said, picking up the briefcase. "You'll want to settle in properly, no doubt."

"By heck!" Poppy exploded when he had gone leaping up the stairs two at a time, his jacket over one arm. "Madam must have given her orders. All lowly staff on the top floor."

Melissa laughed. "Olivia? But she didn't know I'd be needing a room."

"Got everything sussed, that one. Contingency plans, of course. She doesn't let a detail escape that scheming mind of hers."

"You make her sound like a dragon."

"Good description."

"And when shall I be meeting this dragon?"

Poppy shrugged. "She'll come when it suits her."

"I can't wait."

"But don't worry about moving rooms. The mauve one's going spare."

Melissa wasn't about to start questioning her employer's authority at this stage or she'd be out of here like a bullet from a gun. From what she had seen so far of Trailover House she approved. She liked Poppy too, and her warmth and kindness that made her feel at home.

"Come on then, Poppy, why don't you show me where to go?" she said.

This time the view was across to the sea. Melissa was hoping that from this high position, she would catch a glimpse of the ruined village of Trailover but it was out of sight in a dip of the land. On her first day off she would make a beeline for it, but not straight across the firing range area, she reminded herself.

As she turned back to the room, she realised that for the past hour she hadn't thought about Damien once. The pain that was like a knife sticking into her ribs wasn't nearly so sharp. It was still there, of course, but not like it had been at first.

The first guests arrived next day in their small blue car bulging with suitcases. Melissa watched in surprise as suitcase after suitcase was unloaded. The two elderly ladies were beaming as she welcomed them and then bent down to stroke a small white dog on a lead.

"This is Bobbles," one of them said proudly. "And I'm Miss Fletching. Call me Amy, dear. And this is my cousin, Margaret, Mrs Bond."

Melissa shook hands with them both. Poppy appeared at that moment and they carried the suitcases into the hall.

"I'll see it's all delivered to your room," Poppy told them. "Melissa will show you where it is."

On the way along the passage to the large

room on the ground floor, Melissa learned that the two ladies liked to come away together for a few weeks at this time of the year. They always tried to choose somewhere unusual, away from crowded places and where Bobbles would be made welcome.

"We're so lucky this place opened just in time for us," Miss Fletching said. "So beautifully remote, but near the village I once visited as a little girl. Trailover really was a village then with real people living in it. Such a long time ago and I was only a tiny tot at the time. I remember playing on the green by the post office with a large black cat." She gave a tinkling laugh.

Her cousin laughed too. They were an attractive pair, Melissa thought, so tiny and neat with their closely-cropped grey hair and twinkling glasses. They both doted on their Yorkshire terrier who obviously lapped up the attention. Nic had made no objection to the dog staying in their room with them.

"You'll see a big change in the old village of Trailover now," Melissa said. "All the cottages are just shells and I expect the post office is too."

Mrs Bond looked as if she was about to burst into tears. "So very sad," she said.

"Those poor people turned out of their

homes for the war effort," Miss Fletching said.

"I can see you'll want to visit the village as the first thing you do," Melissa said, smiling.

"Oh, yes, dear," Mrs Bond said. "We like a walk and so does Bobbles, don't you, dearie?"

"Ah, here's Poppy with some of your luggage now," Melissa said, preparing to leave. "You'll see the information notices on the door with the times of meals and everything you need to know. I'll leave you to it."

"Melissa, a moment, please."

She looked up, startled at the critical tone of Nic's voice. He was tapping two fingers of his left hand on the breakfast bar.

"Of course," she said, getting up from the kitchen table where she was having a brief rest from checking records on the laptop in her small room adjoining the main office.

"In private."

She followed him across the hall. For a moment he stood at the window of the office, looking out at the sunny yard where the two ladies were exercising Bobbles. Miss Fletching bent to pat his head.

Nic turned, frowning. "I understand you suggested to them an early visit to the ruined village?"

Melissa smiled as she thought of the interest the two ladies had shown in what she had been telling them of how Trailover looked today. Their concern had been touching. "They seemed to care about it so much," she said.

"Was that wise, do you think?"

She looked at him in surprise. "But won't most of the guests want to go there and see it for themselves?"

"Most guests, unless they've been incited otherwise, wait until the designated official times to make their visits."

"You don't mean . . . ?"

"I most certainly do."

"But what happened?" Melissa glanced at the window. Both ladies had wandered towards the rose bed against the far wall. She could almost hear their happy laughter as they watched Bobbles leap up at a butterfly. "They weren't gunned down or anything?" she couldn't resist saying.

Nic's expression hardened. "It's no joking matter. They were stopped before they'd gone far, luckily. I had the duty officer on the phone sounding irate. It's not good enough, Melissa. You hold a position of authority here. You must be careful of what you say."

He had a point, of course, but she didn't like the way he immediately assumed she was in the wrong. She had made an innocent remark to them, that was all, but he accused her of deliberately encouraging guests into doing something they knew was forbidden.

The warning was on all the hotel literature sent to them when they booked. It was also on the notice attached to their bedroom door as well as other notices about the hotel. The unfairness of Nic's attack made her face flame. "You don't seriously think I did it on purpose?"

"Please see that it doesn't happen again."

He left swiftly and Melissa returned to the computer, deep in thought.

"I've put the kettle on," Poppy said. "Time for a coffee?"

Smiling her assent, Melissa followed her into the kitchen and sat down at the table. Poppy, bustling about with mugs and coffee jar, hummed softly to herself.

The scene was so pleasantly tranquil on this sunny June morning that Melissa felt herself relax. She had done well so far this week, acclimatising herself with the routine of running a hotel and all it entailed. She was beginning to feel that she would be able to cope when Nic had to be away.

More guests had arrived yesterday and others were expected this afternoon. These were a group of school friends in their sixties who liked to holiday together each year. Nic was keen to make a good impression so they would wish to come again. Poppy had worked hard on their allotted rooms and the menus, and all was now ready.

Would she still be meeting old friends at their age, Melissa wondered as Poppy pushed a mug of coffee across the table towards her. She accepted a biscuit and bit it thoughtfully. Not Leonie for sure. She shuddered.

The memory of that fateful evening at home, only days before what should have been her special day, shot into her mind so suddenly, she gasped. She had taken the family dog out for his walk on the downs, the stretch of wooded grassland on the summit of the higher ground near her parents' Bristol home.

She knew that Damien had had to rush off to some appointment but had never dreamed that it was with Leonie, her chief bridesmaid-to-be. Or that the appointment could be anything like the scene she was witnessing with such shock and disbelief.

They were sitting in the shelter of a clump of bushes on the edge of the wood. Damien was kissing her.

But now a red mist blurred her vision and there was a drumming in her ears. What sort of man would betray her in that despicable way with her best friend? A man she wanted to spend the rest of her life with? No way!

Her vision clearing, she gazed back at the room, clenching and unclenching her hands, and saw Poppy watching her in concern. Struggling to relax, Melissa tried to smile but the skin was tight round her mouth.

"Are you OK?" Poppy asked, frowning.

Melissa leapt up. "Sorry, Poppy, I've thought of something I must do at once. I'm off to pick some flowers to brighten up the office." She strode out of the kitchen. She needed air and space to calm herself and come to terms with her feelings now.

Outside in the garden, sunlight lit up the golden flowers on the broom on the other side of the stretch of grass. The sweet scent reached out to her as she got near. The flowers were so bright, so cheerful and just the thing needed for the rather dark interior of the room on the ground floor.

She pulled off branches of yellow broom, the tears streaming down her face. Her blaze of anger just now had cleansed her confused thinking. She must hope now that it was the start of a healing process that would continue until all thoughts of him faded for good. No way was she going to let memories of him ruin her life.

She sniffed and rubbed one hand across her face.

"What are you doing with those?" a voice asked.

Startled, she saw that Nic was with her, having come silently across the grass without her knowing.

"What do you want?" she asked.

He smiled. "Do I have to want anything?"

"Well, no." She smiled too, aware that she had sounded abrupt. Damien's behaviour was no fault of Nic's. She held out the broom she had picked. "I hadn't realised they smelled so sweet."

"Lovely, isn't it?" he agreed. "My grandmother's favourite. She loved to see it growing out here but she would never bring it indoors."

"I'm allowed to pick some?"

"Why not? There's plenty there."

She buried her face in the soft flowers in order to cool her burning cheeks. He gave no indication that he had seen her tears and she hoped he hadn't noticed.

"Olivia's arriving this afternoon," he said.

She raised her face. "Does Poppy know?"

He gave a wry smile. "I've just told her."

Melissa knew what Poppy's reaction would be and was glad she hadn't been there to witness it. "I'd better get these in water before they fade," she said.

They walked across the grass, Nic adjusting his long loping strides to suit hers. At the house, he paused and gave her a brief smile. "I can see something's troubling you, Melissa," he said. "Is it anything to do with this place? You would tell me, wouldn't you?"

Mortified, she looked down at the flowers in her hand. "It's all right. It's nothing to do with Trailover. I mean . . . I'm OK now. Nothing I can't cope with."

"Promise?"

"Of course." She wished he would go. She needed to bathe her eyes in cold water and comb her hair. Poppy would see what a mess she looked and want to know the reason. She couldn't bear any sympathy at the moment.

She was aware of the sharp look Nic gave her before leaving her and appreciated his tact in not questioning her further. This was just one little blip and wouldn't happen again. Anything she had once felt for Damien was over.

She went to the cupboard in the back hall where the vases were kept and chose a large cut glass one for the branches of yellow broom. She felt a lightness of heart as if a burden had been lifted from her.

The first day of the rest of my life, she thought as she set about arranging her flowers. She buried her face in their sweet scent once more before carrying them along the hall and into the main office. Facing north, the room needed brightening and her golden flowers made a splash of welcome sunshine on the windowsill.

She heard the front door slam and the sound of loud voices. The next moment the office door burst open.

CHAPTER THREE

Melissa looked round in expectation, knowing that the sounds she had heard outside heralded Olivia's arrival. Nearly every day for the past week she had wondered how Olivia would affect the day-to-day running of the hotel.

Poppy had made no secret of her dislike for her as they discussed the menus for the week ahead. If all she said was true Olivia was likely to be the brains of the place, running it with cold efficiency and expecting her own way in everything without any consideration for the guests' comfort and enjoyment. And what of Nic? Would he allow this sort of thing in his beloved Trailover House? Melissa hadn't thought so but had decided to wait and see.

The door opened. Olivia froze on seeing she was not alone. "Melissa, I take it?" she said, her eyes cold.

"And you must be Olivia," Melissa said.

She moved forward to greet her. "It's good to meet you at last. Did you have a good trip down?"

Olivia stared hard at her. "Reasonably good, no thanks to Nic. He drives as always, like a maniac."

"He does?" Melissa could well imagine that her employer would enjoy putting his foot down. But driving like a maniac? Somehow she didn't think so.

Olivia ran her hand round the neck of her jersey. Melissa had imagined a long-limbed Olivia, groomed to the last inch and dressed as if she was the highest executive in the land. Instead, she was wearing jeans, smartly cut it was true, and a thick jersey far too warm for the time of year. Her dark hair was sleeked back into a knot that gave her face a severity that was strangely attractive.

"So you've already made yourself at home?" Olivia said in an accusing tone.

Melissa stepped back a little. She glanced round the room, noting the neat stack of hotel brochures on the desk near the computer and the empty in-tray. "I'm sure I'll be happy here," she said. She tried hard not to sound defensive as if she was on trial but she simply couldn't help it.

Nic had interviewed and employed her as his personal assistant. There was nothing for her to apologise to Olivia about in being in the office. This was where she should be as she familiarised herself with the business.

"That's all right then," Olivia said grudgingly.

"Of course it's all right," Nic said as he entered the room behind Olivia and smiled at them both. "I'm glad to know you're getting to know each other. I've been filling Olivia in a bit on the way back from the station, Melissa. I'd better find Poppy and get some coffee organised."

"I'll do that for you," Melissa said, anxious to escape.

Before she could move Olivia let out a cry of outrage. "Those flowers!"

Melissa was surprised at the disgust in her voice. "I brought them in to brighten things up and scent the room," she said. "Don't you like them?"

"You've done it on purpose," Olivia cried as she wrenched a paper tissue from her pocket and applied it to her eyes. "Get them out of here at once."

Mortified, Melissa rushed to the window and held the offending vase against her. "You have hay fever? I'm so sorry. I didn't know."

Nic looked taken aback. "My dear, there was no ill intention, I'm sure. It's a simple matter to remove them and no harm done."

Olivia sniffed loudly. The stiff line of her shoulders showed her deep displeasure. "Harm?" she cried. "Of course there's harm done if an employee defies you."

Nic glanced at Melissa, his eyes condemning though she couldn't think why. "It was entirely innocent on Melissa's part, I'm sure."

Olivia tore another tissue from her pocket. "Innocent!" she cried. "Why do you think we have silk flowers in reception?"

Melissa hesitated. She had noticed the arrangement of silk roses behind the desk, of course, and thought it strange not to use fresh ones when they grew in such profusion outside. She had been naïve not to ask the reason. "I'm sorry," she said again.

"Come, my dear," Nic said, taking Olivia's arm and leading her out into the hall as if she was blind. "Ah, Poppy, there you are. Some coffee please in my sitting-room immediately."

They moved away. Melissa, with her vase of sweet-scented broom, stood watching them. She still felt shocked by Olivia's bitter reaction.

"So what was all that about?" Poppy asked when they had gone. "Don't tell me you've fallen out with our Olivia already?"

Melissa smiled weakly. "I did the wrong thing there with the flowers in the office. What a bad start. I didn't know about Olivia's hay fever."

Poppy snorted. "Nor me either."

"The flowers affected her so suddenly."

"Says who?"

"But her eyes were watering, Poppy."

"With spite I shouldn't wonder. Scared you'll get your hands on Nic when she wants him for herself."

"Oh, please."

Poppy indicated the kitchen. "You'll have to watch your back, Melissa. She'll have it in for you now. But bring your flowers in here. By heck, that'll keep madam out of my space."

Melissa, laughing, did as she was told. But it wasn't a laughing matter. She sat down at the table and watched Poppy prepare a tray of coffee things. Had their positions been reversed she would have played her feelings down for the other person's sake however bad the flowers made her feel.

Over-reaction on Olivia's part? Probably. Something else too, that she didn't care to think about. Had Olivia made a fuss merely to embarrass her? She was beginning to suspect that she had.

"Nic didn't mention Olivia's hay fever

when he saw me picking them to bring indoors," she said.

Poppy gave a scornful laugh as she filled the coffee pot. "Forget it, did he? I've never known Nic forget anything."

Melissa was silent. She would know better in future. As soon as she could she would have to find a way to placate Olivia. Bad feeling between them could spoil the calm atmosphere of this place so easily and no-one wanted that. Maybe it would be advisable to keep out of Olivia's way as much as possible.

Melissa's day off each week was Wednesday. Since the first week was a busy one she had elected to forgo any time to herself for the time being.

But then that changed.

"We'll be taking a trip to London soon," Nic told her one morning when she was at the computer printing out new menus for the coming week. "Next week, I think."

She looked up, smiling. He was wearing a suit today instead of his casual sweatshirt and jeans. "So you'll leave me in charge here?"

He looked anxious. "Can you cope, do you think?"

"Of course," she said with confidence. Why should he suddenly have doubts? He made it clear from the beginning that this was part of her job and she had accepted that without question.

In fact she was looking forward to the added responsibility. The thought of it had filled her mind so exclusively that there was little time for brooding about Damien and that was a good thing. She was getting there. "There's no problem surely?" she asked.

"Well, no," Nic said slowly. "A week away, is that too long?"

She shook her head, putting a hand up to smooth her unruly hair. "Hardly. I've had time to get used to what I need to do."

"Well, yes, but taking full responsibility is something else."

"But that's really why I'm here isn't it?"

"As long as you're sure." He moved to the window and picked up the shining paper-weight that Olivia had placed there. He didn't look too certain himself but she couldn't help that.

Last week he had been sure she had the job at her fingertips so what had happened to change his attitude now? A bit of under-mining from Olivia? Yes, definitely. Tight-lipped, Melissa considered. The only thing she could do was to prove to him that she knew her job and could cope with whatever was thrown at her in his absence.

"You need some time off this week to make up for not taking a day off last Wednesday," he said. "Take the rest of today and tomorrow, Melissa. That's what I came in to say."

She smiled. "Thanks. I've nearly finished these, Nic. I want to go down to the village since the road's open today. No red flags in sight."

He looked down at the paperweight in his hand. "That's settled then. I'll tell Olivia."

Her time off could hardly matter to Olivia one way or the other, Melissa thought as she went upstairs for her camera and walking shoes. Since that first day she hadn't seen much of her. Nic, of course, was concerned with office work for a part of each day and checking various things with Poppy. He spent time with the guests too, making sure they enjoyed their stay.

With a feeling of pleasing purpose, Melissa set off along a path that led down across a green hillside and then up again to a higher ridge before sloping gradually downwards to the cliff edge. Beyond, the sea stretched in shimmer calm with a slight haze on the horizon.

She stood for a moment, her eyes half-closed against the brightness, savouring the sunshine on her face and the fresh salty air.

Then she took out her camera and focussed on the gap in the dry-stone wall. Through the gap she could see a ruined tank in the distance half on its side in a ditch. This was an interesting subject for a photograph.

Moving on, she paused at intervals as the beach down below became visible. The jagged headland on the other side of it inspired more photos. Satisfied at last, she ran down the remaining way to the beach. A family group had settled down nearby and the shouts of the children mingled with the crying of seagulls as they swooped high in the air.

The scene was so pleasant Melissa was tempted to stay, but there was much to explore. Had she brought a packed lunch there would have been no problem. Never mind, she could always return this afternoon to make the most of this beautiful place while she had the chance.

Smiling, she turned and saw she was not alone. A large black dog sniffed among the gorse bordering the path that lead inland and his owner bent to release him from his lead. At once the dog ran down to the sand, glad to be free.

"I can let him free at this time of year before it gets too busy," the owner said, seeing Melissa. He threw back his head and

41

shielded his eyes to watch his dog scamper down to the edge of the sea and plunge in.

"He's enjoying himself," Melissa observed. "Have you walked far?"

He nodded as he pushed the lead into the pocket of his shorts. "A fair way. I'm off-duty today. It's a good way to relax."

"Me too," Melissa said. "I'm working up at Trailover House."

"For Nic Haldane? I heard he had a new assistant. You like it there?"

"Very much."

"I'm the range warden here. Craig Hendon. I've been meaning to call at the hotel and see how Nic's getting on these days. Public relations are an important part of my work, as you can imagine." He grinned suddenly and his lined face lit up.

"I'm Melissa Feilden," she said, smiling.

"You've been taking photos?"

"It's my hobby. I thought I'd spend the day exploring the area and practising with my camera. Ideal conditions today."

"Take a look at the local paper, why don't you? They're asking for photos of local scenes. Might be worth a try if you're interested."

"Thanks, I will," she said. She felt warmer, less lonely standing beside this kind stranger.

"You've been to the old village?" he asked.

"That's next on the agenda," she told him.

"Splendid, splendid. You know where it is? Just under a mile inland up this track."

"It sounds a fascinating place."

"It inspires an air of mystery, I agree," he said. "Possibly because access is barred for a lot of the time. There are one or two books on the subject. I know Nic's got some up at the house. In fact I'm researching a book myself at the moment with a slightly different slant."

"Sounds interesting," she said.

He grinned again "I'm studying the family history of some of the families."

His dog's head, a dark dot on the surface of the sea, came rapidly closer. In no time the animal had come lumbering out of the water and was standing shaking himself on the beach.

"Here boy!" Craig gave a whistle.

Melissa smiled to see the dog come running. "Enjoy the rest your walk," she said, preparing to go.

"See you around," he said, his eyes sombre again.

The old village of Trailover was smaller than she had imagined. All the cottages were mere shells of what they had been. She found the one that would have been the post office by the green where Miss Amy Fletching had played as a child. Other children too would have called this place home.

How had they felt when they and their families were told to leave? Excited possibly at going somewhere new but their parents must have been anxious for their immediate future though buoyed up with the promise that they could return when the war ended.

With a saddened heart, Melissa spent some time wandering in and out of the derelict homes, photographing the sightless windows and empty fireplaces. Then she moved round the corner where the church stood. This, a consecrated building, had been lovingly kept up. Opposite the church was the school.

With a feeling of unreality Melissa went inside the restored building, passing rows of named pegs in the passageway before entering the schoolroom. Bemused, she looked at the rows of desk and the exercise books open on each. The writing was old fashioned and beautifully clear. The names on the pegs were old fashioned too . . . Nora, Brenda, Joan and Doreen, Sylvia and Daphne.

There was Dick, two Joes, Bill and two Georges as well as several others more difficult to read.

Seeing the names brought a lump to

Melissa's throat and she rubbed her hand across her eyes as she concentrated on her camera. The labelled pegs made it all so poignant.

On the way back up the lane to Trailover House, Melissa found herself peopling the cottages in her imagination. She tried to imagine where the people had gone when the time came to leave their home village.

She would have to find out about the Trailover villagers. The range warden, Craig Hendon, had said there were books written about it. Trailover House had a well-stocked library. She might well find something there.

In the event she found two, one a thick dry-looking tome and the other more readable with many illustrations that she concentrated on first. The photographs in it showed some of the cottages as they had once been, and then their state in the present day. She pored over the photographs for some time until she heard someone enter the room. She looked up and saw Nic.

"Ah, I see you've found the books about the village," he said as he selected a book from one of the shelves. "What did you think of the place?"

"Sad," she said.

"Oh yes, very. You will have seen my

grandmother's school books in the school-room."

"She was one of the children?" Melissa asked in surprise.

"Joan Lambert, nine years old. I've been meaning to do a bit of research about her. She never talked much about her time in the village. I was very fond of her and she of me. I bought this house because of her, you know, and decided to make a success of the hotel business here in her memory. She'd have liked to have known about me coming here to settle down." He looked pensively at the book in his hand, seemed about to say more but then stopped as Olivia came into the room.

"You found it?" she asked, ignoring Melissa.

Nic held up the book. "Here it is."

"Good-oh. We're all set then."

"We have to be in London tomorrow," Nic said. "Short notice I'm afraid."

Olivia gave Melissa a brilliant smile. "Is that a problem?"

Nic looked at her closely. "I must stress, Melissa, that you should be on the premises at all times while we're away."

She nodded. "Of course." He meant it she could see. Fire and brimstone if she sneaked off on some ploy of her own. So there went her time off. "No problem at all," she said. "Will you be away long?"

"Several days," Olivia said, looking at Nic.

He nodded. "I'll be in touch each day," he said. He sounded indifferent now and in a hurry to be off.

As they went out Olivia looked back with such an expression of triumph that Melissa almost recoiled. But then she told herself to ignore it. She was here to do a job and she would do it well.

CHAPTER FOUR

The back door creaked shut behind Melissa after breakfast next morning. She must remember to tell Ted so he could attend to it when he next came in to do odd jobs.

The clouds beginning to mass on the horizon looked ominous, but there was time, surely, to dash across the grass to pick some of the roses in the bed on the other side for her own room now that Olivia wasn't here to object. She wasn't leaving the grounds so Nic wouldn't disapprove, and she had her mobile with her.

She ran across the lawn with the kitchen scissors in her hand. Wet weather was definitely forecast and this might be her last chance before rain damaged the delicate pink petals.

Hastily she cut some stems, glancing back over her shoulder as the distant sound of gunfire from the ranges was obliterated suddenly in a rumble of thunder. A dog barked.

An eerie silence followed. The clouds now looked like angry mountains of darkness approaching over the sea.

Poppy would call her a fool for lingering out here but the storm was coming faster than she anticipated. She had always liked storms. Leonie was always frightened and used to cling to her for comfort sometimes on the way home from primary school even when the thunder was distant as it was now.

Where was Leonie at this moment . . . she and Damien? Melissa paused in her snipping to wonder. Would the time ever come when thinking of them together didn't fill her with bitter pain? She must try harder to make such an interesting life for herself here so that she no longer thought of them. She needed new friends, new interests and had made a good start here with Poppy.

A spot of rain fell, and then more. The wind blew fiercely in the trees. Clutching her roses, Melissa ran. As she reached the kitchen door her mobile rang. She rushed inside, her hair dripping, and clicked it on. "Hello?"

"Melissa is that you? You sound strange."

"Damien?" she gasped. "What is it? What do you want?" His voice was warm, reassuring, but she wasn't reassured. She looked down at the water gathering at her feet. "I can't talk now. Or ever."

"Please, Melissa. I'm missing you."

"No, no way," she stressed. She had made her decision.

"Mel, listen to me. We have to talk."

All she wanted at the moment was to get into something dry. She had got over her first shock of betrayal with some difficulty. She didn't need this now. "I can't talk now."

"Later then."

"Not even then. It's finished Damien. Let it go."

She switched off her mobile and stood leaning against the kitchen table. The storm had been fierce and sudden. The rain had stopped now but the trees near the house were bending wildly this way and that. She stared through the glass panel of the door at the clouds whipping past.

Behind her the door into the hall burst open under the thrust of Poppy's shoulder. The pile of sheets she was clutching she let fall on the table and looked at Melissa in alarm.

"Is owt wrong?"

Melissa bit her lip and rubbed her arm across her wet hair. "I was out picking flowers when the rain came." She was still clutching her roses and she raised them to her face to breathe in their sweet scent before placing them carefully on the table as if they were the most precious things in the world.

"And?" Poppy sighed.

Melissa sighed. "I must get changed." Instead of moving she collapsed into a chair and put her head in her hands. "Oh Poppy, I thought he'd gone for good and would leave me alone. I can't talk to him anymore, I can't."

"Happen he'll get the message," Poppy said as she picked up the flowers and reached beneath the sink for a glass container to put them in. "Whoever he is." She swung round and stared hard at Melissa.

"Damien rang me on my mobile," Melissa said, feeling wretched.

"Tell me about it," Poppy said, sitting down too. "I'm a right good listener."

It was calming somehow, to pour it all out to someone whom she knew would be sensible as well as sympathetic. Melissa told how she and Damien had been close for at least two years before they started to plan the wedding and make their plans for the future together.

Seeing him with Leonie had shocked her into immobility for what had seemed like hours. "Only a few minutes really," she said, pushing her damp hair away from her face.

"When I went rushing home I didn't know what to do. Then he phoned."

"And what did he say?"

"Nothing much. That was the terrible thing. Only that it had come on them suddenly and they couldn't seem to help themselves."

"The rat," Poppy said suddenly. "You hadn't noticed owt wrong?"

Melissa shook her head. "What sort of fool does that make me?"

"Trusting and loving, that's all."

Melissa shivered. "How could I go through with the wedding after that?"

"He still wanted to?"

"I don't know. I still don't know. But I don't want to see him any more."

"And your friend?"

"Vanished out of my life. That hurt too. We'd known each other from when we were babies. She was my best friend, or so I thought. She never gave a hint about caring for Damien. She seemed happy for us." Melissa buried her face in her hands again.

She raised her face and stood up. "Thanks Poppy. I must go and change."

"There'll be a hot drink waiting for you when you get back," Poppy promised.

Standing under the shower, Melissa found the hot stream of water comforting. She had thought she was going so well in pushing Damien to the back of her mind until her mobile had leapt alive as she reached the safety of the house. But how safe was she at Trailover if Damien could reach her so easily when she had thought she had got him out of her life? She didn't even know where he was . . . abroad still?

By the same token he didn't know where she was either as her parents had been sworn to secrecy and no-one else knew. That was the best of mobiles. Or the worst.

Later she would phone him and make it crystal clear she wanted nothing more to do with him, now or ever.

For the rest of the morning, Melissa worked hard. There were records to enter on computer, and one of their suppliers to contact before sending out some more copies of the prospectus to likely future clients.

When this was done she plugged in her camera and loaded her photos so she could view them on screen. She had thought she would submit the one of Trant Castle to the paper but then hesitated. The photo of the derelict tank definitely had something.

She printed it out and was pleased with the result. It could go off in the post this morning. Deleting the photos on screen, she unplugged the camera and closed down the computer.

Sounds of agitation were coming from outside. Miss Fletching and her cousin were in the hall, looking troubled.

"Oh my dear," Miss Fletching cried. "He hasn't come back then? Oh we did hope he had. We've been out looking. We can't find him."

"Bobbles?" Melissa asked in alarm. She frowned. "When did you last see him?"

"We let him out before breakfast," Mrs Bond said. "We always do, don't we, Amy?"

"Always." Her cousin nodded. "It was such a nasty morning. Oh, Margaret should we look again?"

Melissa thought of the bark she had heard at the first rumble of thunder. It came from the direction of the ranges. Could it have been Bobbles? "Where have you been looking? Not on the ranges with the red flags flying?"

"Oh no, dear." Amy Fletching looked anxious. "Well, only a little way in. We did no harm. Margaret will tell you."

"You really mustn't," Melissa said as calmly as she could. "The ranges are strictly out of bounds." She should really lay down the law and make them understand the importance of staying off anywhere likely to be dangerous. But now was not the right moment with the two of them so anxious about poor Bobbles.

Margaret Bond pulled out a dainty lace hanky and dabbed at her eyes. "Poor little Bobbles."

"I'd better phone the range warden's office," Melissa said.

She got through at once and spoke to the girl on the other end of the phone. She was thoughtful as she replaced the phone on the receiver. "She said that no dog has been found but she'll report it," she said. "I hope I've done the right thing."

"I'm sure you have, dear," Amy Fletching said, pulling away from Poppy and giving her a brilliant smile before looking hopefully at Melissa. "We'd better take another look outside, hadn't we, Margaret?"

"You'll keep off the ranges?"

"Of course, dear."

"Has Bobbles done this sort of thing before?" Melissa asked.

"Well yes," Amy admitted apologetically. "He's a naughty boy. He always comes back in the end, you know, and no harm done."

Melissa sighed and looked away. No harm usually but what about this time? A written report about the incident might harm Trailover Hotel's reputation. She sighed again as the two ladies left to continue their search.

The two new guests arrived just before lunch and in behind them came the two ladies with a bedraggled little white dog in tow.

"Bobbles," Melissa cried in delight, and had to explain to the bewildered Colonel and Mrs Beale exactly why she was so pleased. As she showed them to their room on the first floor she told them some more about the two ladies because they were so interested.

"Marjorie is fond of dogs," the colonel said, looking at his wife affectionately. "I think we shall find we have a lot in common."

Melissa agreed. The two ladies both dressed formally at all times and it seemed as if these two would approve of that. The Colonel, stooping a little, had the air of old-fashioned courtesy about him. Mrs Beale's skirt was unfashionably long and she wore her greying hair in a bun in the nape of her neck.

In the days that followed they were continually seen together.

"He's having the time of his life," Melissa told Poppy one day when they had finished sorting out the menus for the following week and Melissa was preparing to go into the office to do a print-out on the computer.

The phone rang. Melissa hesitated. There was always this second of apprehension now. Absurd to think that Damien would know the hotel number, but there it was. "I'll take it in the office," she said.

There was coolness in Nic's voice on the other end of the line. Melissa, relieved it was her boss phoning for his daily report, didn't notice at first. There was little to tell him except that everything was running smoothly.

Then she thought of Colonel Beale and thought it might amuse Nic to know how well some of his guests were mixing with each other even though today the Colonel had gone off to spend time with his old army friend at his home in Poole until to-morrow.

There was a moment's silence when she finished. "Anyway, how are you, Nic? Is your business nearly finished?" she added.

"I'll be home in the next day or two," he said.

She had to be content with that.

Melissa woke suddenly and glanced at her watch. Five o'clock and only just beginning to get light. Was that a sound in the passageway outside? She got out of bed and reached for her dressing-gown and mobile phone.

A tap came on the door. "Melissa, dear, are you awake?"

She rushed to open the door. "What is it?" she asked, seeing Margaret Bond in her mauve nightgown with her hair loose about her stricken face. "What's wrong?"

The older woman clutched her hands together. "My dear, we didn't want to disturb you but we feel you really must come."

"Of course." Melissa shut her bedroom door behind her.

"It's Marjorie. She's ill," Margaret Bond said with a gasp, as she hurried ahead of Melissa along the passage and made for the staircase. "She's in terrible pain and her husband's not here. Oh why did he have to be away just at his time?"

"The lift," Melissa said firmly, taking her elbow and guiding her towards it. This was out of bounds during the night and early hours but this was an exception.

Amy Fletching, hovering near the bed, gave a little squeak when they went in. By the light of the table lamp Melissa saw that Marjorie Beale's face was ashen-white. Her forehead was burning hot and her hand dry.

"I'll phone the emergency services,"

Melissa said.

"Oh, yes," Amy Fletching said.

"Could you get a few things together for her?" she asked the two ladies when she had done so. She could see that their fussing was worrying the patient who clutched for her own hand.

"Don't leave me," she whispered.

"I won't," Melissa promised. "I'll be back as quickly as I can, don't worry. The ambulance will be here soon so I'll need to get some clothes on."

She was back within minutes, thankful she had left her jeans and sweatshirt handy on her bedroom chair. She pulled a comb through her hair as she came back into the room.

The poor woman looked terrible. Her husband must be informed as soon as she could reach him. Maybe when they were on their way in the ambulance. Because of course she would go too because the patient was begging her. This was an emergency and she must use her initiative.

"Can you wake Poppy and put her in the picture?" she asked Margaret Bond. "Tell her I'll be back as soon as I can."

Colonel's Beale's number? Too much to expect that he had a mobile. To her relief Amy Fletching had located Marjorie's handbag and pressed it into her hand.

There would surely be an address book or something inside. She would do the best she could.

In the event it was easy, and Colonel Beale was soon contacted. He arrived at the hospital a bare half hour after his wife was carried in. He found Melissa in the hospital waiting area.

"It was good of you, my dear," he said, pressing Melissa's hand warmly. "Thank you for taking care of her."

Appendicitis, they were told. And not to worry. She was in good hands.

"I must get back," Melissa said when they had drunk the coffee the Colonel got from the machine. "I'll phone for a taxi."

"No need." Colonel Beale placed his paper cup on the table and stood up. "I'll run you back. Something to so while she's on the operating table."

To her dismay she saw Nic's Volvo near the front door. This could only mean trouble for her. He was lifting his laptop from the back seat, looked up and saw her. For a moment a disbelieving expression flickered across his face.

She swallowed hard and threw back her shoulders, determined not to let him brow beat her before she had a chance to explain.

"Good morning, Nic."

His brows drew closer together as he nodded a greeting. His dark suit gave him an air of sternness. His dark blue tie must be tight because he loosened it as she came near. "You left the premises." It was a statement rather than a question.

"I was dealing with an emergency," she said. "I left Poppy in charge."

He slammed shut the car door. "You did?" His voice was calm, controlled. "I need to hear more of this."

He stood aside and she entered the house before him. The hall was silent and felt cold. Where was Poppy? The roses on the desk seemed to stand out in defiance but he barely glanced at them as he lowered his suitcase to the floor and placed his laptop on the desk. "Explain!"

Melissa did so, stating the bald facts and trying not to let her voice falter at Nic's hard expression. He plainly thought she was in the wrong but how could she have let the poor woman down when she so plainly needed her?

"It was emergency," she said. "I dealt with it the best way I could."

"The ambulance crew are trained to cope," he said crisply. "There might well have been a crisis here in your absence. Had you considered that? You know the rules. I expected you to keep them."

"I had to take the risk," she said faintly.

"Had something occurred with neither of us here the insurance might well have been invalid," he said. "It could mean the ruin of us."

There was nothing she could say to that except to apologise and she wasn't about to do that. Couldn't he see she had no choice? It was unfeeling of him not to have even asked after the patient. Not that she could have told him much at this stage of course. But his cold reaction didn't help her.

"It was irresponsible and stupid," Nic said. There was a tight line round his mouth and his eyes looked hard. "We need to talk more of this. Go now and get some rest. I'll see you later."

Melissa went upstairs to her room, hardly realising how she got there. She fell on her bed and closed her eyes. She must have slept because when she opened them again the sun was well up.

Hastily she showered and in a change of clothes felt better. Apart from the distant humming of the vacuum cleaner in one of the downstairs rooms all was quiet.

In the kitchen Poppy had left a tray ready for her with a note propped against the coffee pot. *Melissa, help yourself to what you want. Colonel B. has come back. All well with Mrs. Nic's in the office. Wants to see you pronto. Good luck, girl.*

Poppy was a pal. Melissa smiled as she sipped her coffee. She reached for a banana from the fruit dish and peeled it. Sunlight reflecting on the electric kettle looked cheerful. She would be cheerful too. She tossed the banana skin in the pedal bin and carried her coffee mug to the sink to wash it.

Sacked for a kind deed, that was something. Sacked for irresponsibility, well that was something else.

CHAPTER FIVE

Nic was on the phone with his back to her as Melissa went in. She closed the door behind her and waited, feeling like a wayward pupil in the headmistress's study.

"I'll get her to call you then," she heard him say. "She knows your number no doubt. 'Bye, then."

Damien again? A faint feeling of dizziness swept over her. She clutched the edge of the desk, fearing she would faint.

Replacing the receiver, Nic turned. She raised her eyes and met his, hoping he didn't see the fear she was sure was showing in her own.

"That was Craig Hendon," he said. "He's seen the paper. He wants you to get in touch. He's off somewhere at the moment but he'll be back in about ten minutes if you'd like to call him then."

She stared at Nic blankly. This wasn't making sense. What had Craig to do with

Damien? "What paper?" she said faintly.

"Craig's seen your photo in the local rag. He's impressed. He'd like to discuss the likelihood of you doing some photos for him. You know he's writing a book?"

The blood seemed to rush out of Melissa's head and then back again. She took a deep breath, feeling stupid.

"Here, take a seat," Nic said. He pulled forward a chair and she sat down. Her head was clearing now and she could think straight again.

Nic seated himself at the computer and swivelled his chair so he was facing her. "Do you think it's a good idea or would it all be a bit much?"

"I'll phone him," she said.

He nodded. "You've nothing to lose." He picked up a pen and clicked it on and off. Apart from that there was silence for a moment.

"Colonel Beale has contacted us," he said at last. "All is well with his wife. She's back in the ward now and he's on his way back here for a few hours. He was full of praise for you, Melissa. I'm still concerned about your leaving the premises, but I can see that in the circumstances there was no help for it." He put down the pen and straightened the cuff of his dark green sweatshirt, a faint smile tugging at his lips.

Melissa smiled too, thankful that he had come to see her side of things. Poor Colonel Beale was mortified not to have been here and would be devastated if she was in deep trouble because of it.

Nic seemed more relaxed now, thank goodness. Obviously this was as much of an apology as he was going to make but it was enough.

"Hopefully this was a one-off," she said. "I'll try not to let it happen again." She was surprised by his quizzical expression. Was he expecting that she would do exactly that and already planning what to do about it? "What would have happened in an emergency before I came?" she asked.

He frowned. "There were two of us working here then," he said.

He and Olivia? Did that mean Olivia no longer wished to be part of the running of the hotel? Poppy had said that Olivia had a financial stake in Trailover. Where was she now anyway?

Nic turned his chair, pushed the telephone on the desk farther from him and stood up. "Miss Fletching and Mrs Bond have been talking to me too."

Melissa got to her feet too. "They have?"

"Another case of trespassing on the

ranges, I hear."

Her face felt warm. Oh dear, what had the ladies been saying? "Not for long and not very far," she said quickly. "They did no harm."

"The dog ran off, I gather. He must be kept under control at all times. That's the rule."

"They know that, Nic."

He smiled again, suddenly. "Don't worry, they stressed how good and understanding you had been about it. They are all at it, standing up for you."

Humbled, Melissa could only agree. She didn't know why this was but it gave her a warm feeling round her heart. She felt an awkward smile flicker on her lips and then die.

He gestured towards the door. "I won't keep you then. You'd better have the rest of the morning off after your disturbed night. No doubt you've plenty to do. You'll get in touch with Craig?"

She nodded. "Thanks, Nic." He seemed concerned that she should do this. Weak tears came to her eyes as she left. She hadn't expected kindness. It was almost too much after the trauma of the night and Nic's unexpected return.

But there was a lot to consider before she

rang Craig. Suppose the rest of her photos didn't come up to scratch? Would she have time to take another set if so? She ran upstairs to unzip her camera from its bag to view the results again.

"One minute, Melissa!"

Melissa paused as Olivia appeared on the first floor landing. Her dark hair was even more strained back from her pale face than usual. One glance was enough to see that Olivia wasn't pleased.

"So there's been trouble again?" she said in a clipped tone. "Obviously things go lax when we're not here. You should never have given permission for the dog to run free outside. Power going to your head, Melissa, and it doesn't do. It's asking for trouble. You should know that by now."

Melissa opened her mouth to reply but before she could speak there was a commotion along the passageway as the two ladies came tripping along, one behind the other. Miss Fletching, in front, held Bobbles on a lead and her face lightened into a smile as she saw Melissa.

"There, my dear. How nice you look today, doesn't she, Margaret? And after your sleepless night too. That blue shirt suits you, dear, and looks so well with your white trousers."

Olivia gave a gesture of annoyance and made to move away but the two ladies were blocking her exit.

Margaret Bond stooped to stroke Bobbles. "A heroine, that's what she is," she said, straightening and looking Olivia in the eye. "Don't you agree? Our Melissa gives this place real class."

This was definitely not what Olivia wanted to hear. Melissa almost expected the ground to shake with the enormity of the words.

Miss Fletching smiled in agreement. "Indeed, that's right. I don't know what you would do here without her."

Melissa was aware that Olivia was still trying to edge past. Obviously she didn't want to waste any more time listening to such rubbish.

"Olivia's trying to get through," she said.

"Oh dear," Miss Fletching said. "We're so sorry. We're just going, aren't we, Margaret?"

With little murmurings of apology, the ladies left.

Olivia's frown was like a threatening storm. "I'm beginning to think you're not suited here, Melissa. You give every sign of irresponsibility. Nic and I have been discussing this. I thought I should warn you."

She flounced off and Melissa stared after

her, dismayed. She had made an enemy of Olivia and there seemed little she could do about it. Nic had said nothing about wanting her to leave and she didn't believe it, but even so, the fact that this was in Olivia's fevered imagination wasn't exactly reassuring.

Before she could put off something she was dreading, Melissa reached for her mobile on her bedside table. Sitting on the edge of her bed, she dialled Damien's mobile.

He answered at once. "Melissa!"

The blood flew to her face as she heard his voice all those miles away. But what if he wasn't miles away but nearby . . . at Trant Magna for instance, and within easy reach of getting here? Don't be stupid, she told herself. She cleared her throat. "I just want to make something quite clear, Damien," she said quickly. "Please don't contact me any more."

"So what's the weather like down there with you?" he said as if she hadn't spoken.

She glanced involuntarily out of the window as if the blue sky and scudding clouds were a surprise to her. "Down where?" she said faintly.

"So you decided to take up the job after

all," he said easily. "How are you settling in?"

She felt suddenly cold. "Where are you, Damien?"

"The hopes of a job in Belgium didn't work out. I was let down badly there so I came back."

No mention of Leonie and she wouldn't ask. Thinking of Leonie was too painful. She took a deep breath. "So where . . . ?"

"In the frozen north, I'm afraid."

"Then please stay there," she said with more spirit. "You heard me. We've nothing more to say to each other now or ever. Please believe that."

"But we're still friends?"

"Friends!" she cried.

"I want to see you again, Melissa."

"But why . . ." she began but then broke off. What was the use of getting into reasons now? "Goodbye, Damien. I'm switching my mobile off now and that's the end of it."

She put it back on the bedside table and sat staring at it for some minutes. Then it began to sink in that she hadn't denied that she had come to Trailover. He knew where she was. Surely he wouldn't seek her out when she had made it plain she didn't want to see him?

Olivia's bitter words about her lack of

responsibility still stung. As did her insinuations that both she and Nic wanted her out of here.

Melissa got up from the bed and moved to the window. The day was still as bright and windy as it had been before she phoned Damien. Nothing had changed.

She would stay here and fight. No way would she give Olivia the satisfaction of seeing her go.

She clicked open her camera and pressed the switch to reveal the viewing screen.

Examining the photos now ultra-critically, she thought they had something about them. She would be able to tell better when they were printed out and perhaps enlarged, but first she would phone Craig and hear what he had to say.

Craig's friendly voice washed soothingly over her bruised heart. He was delighted to hear she would agree to let him have a look at her photos of Trailover and the surrounding area she had already taken, and perhaps take more as time went on.

His book was in its early stages at the moment and more ideas of places to include might well occur. She would be duly acknowledged in the book, of course, when it was published. It all sounded really good.

"I've got a supply of photographic paper,"

she said. "I'll have a go at printing some more out. See what you think."

"Excellent, excellent," he said. "We'll need to meet and look at them together and discuss other suitable subjects in the area. I'll wait to hear from you then."

Melissa was smiling as she ran downstairs again. Nic was still in the office, busy on the computer. He was whistling between his teeth and stopped when he saw Melissa.

"Back again already?" he said, raising his eyebrows.

"There's something I'd like to ask you," she said.

She hesitated, feeling a little awkward now that it came to the point. Was she taking advantage of the good mood Nic was in? Well yes, but why not? It was no good coming out with her request when he was in the middle of an argument with Olivia or had his mind on some problem. "I would like to print out my photos on this printer," she said. "It's ideal for the quality I need."

"You've spoken to Craig?"

"He's keen to see them and to talk business."

"Fine. Give me thirty minutes and then the computer and printer are all yours. As long as you've got free time, feel free to do it when you like."

"I'll cover all expenses of course."

"No need."

"Thanks, Nic," she said as she withdrew for the second time.

With half an hour to kill she sought Poppy out to tell her, and found her humping the laundry basket out of the back door into the sunny garden. Melissa picked up the peg bag and followed.

"Maybe I'll go down to the village again later and take some more shots," she told Poppy as she helped peg sheets on the line.

Poppy reached for another towel from the basket. "So Nic says you can use the computer in the office? Good for you, girl."

"As long as it's in my free time."

"What free time?" Poppy said scornfully. "You get precious little of that with the two of them away."

"Be fair, Poppy. They've only been away once so far," Melissa pointed out.

Nic and Olivia were here now and she had the rest of the day to herself. She must check there were spare colour cartridges, too, and order some more to replace them.

"You look like someone who's lost a penny and found a five pound note," Poppy remarked as they finished the task and she heaved up the empty laundry basket. "Go on with you now and get started. I'll keep back the hordes of fawning guests from bothering you."

Melissa was still smiling when she went in to the office. To have been given the opportunity to do something like this was wonderful. It was the perfect way to keep her mind off the things she was struggling to forget.

Three quarters of an hour later, Melissa sought out Poppy's company once again, eager to show her the results.

"Look," she cried, on finding her in the conservatory. "They've worked out well."

Poppy swung round, a feather duster in her hand. "Show me then."

Melissa spread out her photographic prints on the wicker table and stood back to let her see. Poppy poured over them, her small pinched face alight with interest.

"What do you think?" Melissa asked, impatient to know the verdict.

"That's the best one," Poppy said, pointing to the photograph Melissa had taken of the restored school building.

Melissa was disappointed in her choice. This photograph could have been taken anywhere and didn't illustrate the atmosphere of the ruined village in any way. She pointed to another that showed a view of the church through the open jagged walls of one of the derelict cottages. With this she had got the shadows just right to create the sombre mood she wanted. It almost made her shudder now to see it but Poppy seemed unmoved.

Poppy wrinkled her nose. "You could get a better one if you stood right in front of the church."

"I was after something different, unique," Melissa said.

"I see," Poppy said doubtfully. "Take no notice of me, Melissa. What do I know?" She picked up her feather duster and waved it in the air.

"Watch what you're doing with that," came Olivia's crisp voice. "I thought I heard voices in here."

Poppy scowled. "I'll be off then."

Melissa wished she could escape as easily, but Olivia was looking with curiosity at her display of photographs. "What are these?"

"The results from my digital camera," Melissa said as she began to collect them together.

"You got them printed out?"

"From Nic's computer."

Olivia's eyes narrowed. "Our computer. So you took it in your head to use our property when our backs were turned?"

"With Nic's permission," Melissa said, holding back a sharp retort with difficulty. Olivia's attitude was totally out of order.

"Nic allowed you to do it?" Olivia said swiftly. "When exactly?"

"Not long ago," Melissa said. "And now if you will excuse me there is something I need to do."

Olivia flushed. "Is there indeed?"

Tight-lipped, Melissa left the conservatory, glad that she had managed to keep her temper under control. It seemed that Olivia was still going out of her way to put her in the wrong. Well, let her. Why should she mind her having the use of the computer when no one else needed it?

As usual she was doing what she liked best . . . being awkward. All the same Melissa would have given a lot to know what Olivia honestly thought of her photographs. Nic too, though she knew that his disliking them would hurt in a way Poppy's honest opinion hadn't.

CHAPTER SIX

Craig's house was tucked away off the lane that led down to Trant Magna. Melissa drove carefully, aware that she could easily miss it though she had learnt Poppy's instructions off by heart.

She saw there was no front garden, but only large uncultivated patches at either side. Red flags flew close to the property, streaming out in the wind. To remind Craig of his duties as range warden, she supposed as she parked the car and got out.

He threw open the front door. "Come in, come in," he said. "Bit of a mess, I'm afraid." He grinned at her, running his hand through his mop of greying hair so that some of it stood up in peaks.

Melissa could see that the place was cluttered with coats, anoraks and piles of newspapers. The high window on one side was so smeary she wondered that light could penetrate.

He led the way into the study, a large room on the ground floor. Bookcases lined two walls and a computer and printer stood on a large table in the middle of the room. Filing cabinets took up most of the space on the other walls on either side of the windows. Here everything looked under control and businesslike.

"Here, sit down," he said, removing a pile of books from a chair near the table and seating himself on another one. "Let's see what you've got for me."

She produced the photographs.

He rubbed his hands down the sides of his sweater. "Excellent, excellent," he said as he took them. He got up and carried them across to the window, fortunately clear, and examined them closely. "You've certainly got a talent." He brought them back to the table again and sat down.

Melissa smiled. It was good to have Craig's approval.

"Can I keep these?" he asked.

"You think some of them will do?"

He smiled. "Brilliant. You're a pal, Melissa. Nic thought this would be a good idea, our working together and he was right."

Melissa was surprised. "Nic suggested it?"

Craig flicked through the photographs again. "He's been interested in my project from the first. I get the impression he'd have liked to get involved in some of the research and I'd have been glad to have his help. Out of the question, though. No time since the hotel opened. That's important to him, running the hotel."

Melissa nodded, thinking of what Nic had told her about his grandmother living in the doomed village as a child and about his wish to make a success of the hotel in her memory. She handed Craig the folder in which she had brought the prints. "If you'd like me to photograph anything else for you let me know," she said.

"Of course, of course," he said. "And we'll talk money sometime. Coffee?"

"I must get back," she said regretfully.

He didn't try to detain her. Obviously he needed to get on with what he was doing and she planned to drive down to the village now and have another look round.

She had forgotten the red flags showing that firing was in progress and the road was closed. Ah well, change of plan. She put the car into gear and headed towards Trant Magna and the castle on the hill that had so intrigued her on the day she arrived.

So much had happened since that first day though it was only a few weeks ago. It occurred to her as she drove down the narrow lane that she hadn't thought of Damien for hours.

The village of Trant Magna felt familiar as she drove into the same car park she had used before. Later she would visit the castle, but first she would wander round the narrow cobbled streets and take a proper look at the place.

She came across a small museum so tucked away between taller stone buildings she almost missed it. Intrigued, she pushed open the door. The man in charge looked up from the artefacts he was rearranging on one of the shelves.

"Is it all right if I take a look?" Melissa asked.

"Of course, my dear, feel free." His crinkled face lit up with good humour. "No charge."

Melissa moved slowly round the room, looking at everything with keen interest. There seemed to be a lot of small household things here from Victorian times and earlier. Later, too.

"Oh," she exclaimed, looking closely at a shelf on the far wall. Here was arranged a selection of blue and white pottery plates, saucers and a couple of cups. Alongside was a notice explaining that they had been found in the deserted village of Trailover at the end of the Second World War. Most of them were faded and chipped but Melissa gazed at them as if they were made of the finest bone china.

She felt the man come to stand behind her, no doubt attracted by her interest.

"A strange collection, my dear," he said.

She swung round. "Are there any other things that came from Trailover?" she asked.

"There's not a lot on display," he said, rubbing one hand up and down on the other arm. "Not much room you see. There's that little collection of silver ornaments over there."

Melissa moved across to look. Five little silver dwarfs were displayed in an open velvet box. "They're pretty."

"Charming, aren't they? They were donated soon after the war, but they've only just been put out on display. They belonged to someone at the Rectory, but the owner disliked them after they'd been stolen by some child and then recovered, so that's why we've got them. Anything to do with the school was taken there when they restored the building. You'll have seen it?"

"Oh yes, and I want to go again."

"The rest of the artefacts are stored in the back room. Not much, of course, but people find them of interest."

"What sorts of things are there?"

"Some items of furniture that weren't owned by the tenants, one or two things that got left behind no doubt by mistake, a teddy bear . . ."

"That's dreadful," Melissa said, shocked. "Can I see them? I've brought a notebook. I'll make some notes too."

He shook his head. "Sadly, no. The curator has to give written permission and he's not available at the moment. Another day perhaps?"

Melissa nodded, her mind on the abandoned teddy bear. She would certainly come back on her next day off. What other fascinating items might be hidden away? "Would you object if I took photos?"

"Go ahead, my dear." He moved away to greet a man and a girl who appeared reluctant to enter until he encouraged them inside.

Melissa snapped shut her notebook and got out her camera. Craig might find these of interest and there was no harm in taking them just in case. "Thanks. I'll be back another day," she called as she finished, giving him a brief wave.

Thoughtfully she wandered up to the castle. She paid the entrance fee, picked up an information leaflet and began to walk up the steep path that led up to the ruins.

Had Craig visited the museum and seen all the things there that had come from Trailover? Of course he had. Anyone researching the place would have done that. The wonder was that there was anything left after all these years.

She thought of the silver dwarfs, the chipped pottery and the teddy bear some child had left behind. These things brought the sadness of it all sharply home to her in a way that even visiting the derelict cottages hadn't.

On impulse she pulled out her phone and tapped in Craig's mobile number. She heard the amusement in his voice when she had told him of her visit to the museum.

There was the sound of rattling in the background and a hiss of wind. So he was somewhere outside, perhaps involved in something important. She was sorry she had bothered him.

"Great, great," he said with enthusiasm. "Glad you're interested, Melissa. The village is open for visiting this afternoon, by the way. Make an appointment to see inside the forbidden room, why don't you? Great stuff."

The sound of raised voices greeted her as she opened the front door. Nic and Olivia? They were in the office. Through the slit of the partly-opened door she could hear them clearly. It sounded rancorous and she paused, embarrassed.

Olivia was having a go at Nic and he was responding with such vigour she was sure they could be heard from all the main rooms. Hopefully the guests were still out. Where was Poppy? No doubt hiding away somewhere looking forward to filling her in on all the sordid details.

"I want you with me in London, Nic," Olivia was saying. "Do you understand? A break will do us both good and there's nothing to hold you here. I don't know what you see in the place, I really don't and neither do you if you're honest. You've got a fixation with this place. It's time you grew up.

"Can't we divide the time equally between the two and get a manager in now we've set things up here? Someone with authority. In fact, it's time we sold out and set up somewhere else. Not London if you're against the place. Somewhere else if you like. What could be more reasonable than that?"

Nothing if you hadn't got deep-seated reasons for staying at Trailover, Melissa thought. She couldn't hear Nic's reply but whatever it was inflamed Olivia. Her voice rose. There was the sound of something heavy being dropped.

Suddenly Melissa realised she shouldn't be listening to this. She knew they disagreed over this issue, but not that it had become so acrimonious. Nic was holding his own but she could hardly bear the thought of the deep hurt he must be feeling.

She tried to slip away but as she passed the desk the phone rang. She snatched it up. Wrong number. She replaced the receiver as quietly as she could and moved towards the staircase. The raised voices followed her as she began to ascend and then the office door flew open and slammed shut again.

The peace of her own room was wonderful and she had much to think about. She lay on her bed, her hands behind her head. Would Nic give in and do as Olivia wanted? Her powerful personality made her difficult to withstand, but Nic seemed to have been doing it.

When all had been quiet for fifteen minutes Melissa ventured downstairs again to find the museum's telephone number.

Olivia was seated at the reception desk. On seeing Melissa she looked up. "So . . . who telephoned?"

"Wrong number," Melissa said.

"Were you skulking out here in the hall for long?" Olivia's voice was icy cold and her eyes were hard.

"I'd just come in. I want the museum's phone number. I'm doing some photographic work for Craig Hendon in my spare time."

"So that's where you've been?"

"Is that a problem?"

"You know he's a married man?"

Melissa flushed. "Separated, Poppy said. That had nothing to do with it."

Olivia raised her eyebrows. "No?"

"The museum leaflets have gone. Have you tidied them away?"

"So you've been to that house of his? Alone."

She made it sound like a secret assignation to a love nest, but Melissa wouldn't let her sneering tone get to her. There were other ways of finding the number she wanted. She began to move away.

"I don't think Nic would like the sound of that," Olivia said, standing up. "He's got the good name of the hotel to consider. Did anyone see you?"

Melissa paused. "For goodness sake," she said, annoyed. "I told you. It's a working arrangement. Now, if you'll excuse me . . ."

"Wait!" Olivia placed her hands on the desk and leaned towards her. "I think you should consider leaving here. In fact, I insist. A breath of scandal would be the death of this place and we can't have that."

"And who will spread this alleged scandal?" Melissa said, staring straight into Olivia's eyes.

"No-one if you're sensible. I promise you that. You'll get a good reference if you do as I say and make no trouble."

For a moment Melissa was speechless. Then she turned swiftly and left, closing the front door behind her with a gentleness that took all her willpower. She must be alone. She had to think.

She walked across the lawn to the wooden seat in the shelter of some escallonia bushes that hid it from the house. As she sat down she found she was trembling.

CHAPTER SEVEN

Olivia's voice echoed round and round in Melissa's head. She saw again Olivia's triumphant expression as she came out with something so ridiculous that no-one would surely take it seriously.

The accusations were totally out of order, but they hurt. What she did in her free time was her own affair. No way would she be blackmailed. She and Craig having an affair? The idea was preposterous.

Melissa ran her hands along the wooden arms of the hidden seat, liking the warm smoothness and the feeling of stability it gave her. If Olivia still insisted she left immediately she would refuse to fall in with such an outrageous plan whatever insinuations she threatened to come up with. She gave a strained laugh as she thought about it.

There was no doubt of what Poppy's angry reaction would be. She imagined all too clearly the crashing of pans about in the kitchen and the hurling of abuse at someone she respected about as much as the dirt beneath her feet.

But it wouldn't come to that. The scene just now had left her weakened and upset, that was all. She wouldn't dwell on it a moment longer. Craig was a good friend of Nic's. Incredibly, Nic had suggested she and Craig might work together over the photographs for his book and wasn't about to believe Olivia's wild accusations. She must give herself time to relax and see things in perspective.

Melissa leaned back, aware now of the birdsong in the bushes and trees that shaded this part of the garden. Some wild roses clung to the fence and the scent of honeysuckle hovered in the air which had become still now that the wind had dropped. The only red flag visible from here hung limply on the flagpole.

She would remain here for a further five minutes and then return to the house for lunch. Nic had given her the day off and she would make the most of it.

She would find that telephone number and return to Trant Magna this afternoon while she had the chance. She had worked hard here and would work even harder to make herself indispensable.

A robin appeared at her feet and then, with a flutter of wings, perched on the wooden arm of the seat. She smiled to see his puffed-out chest and beady eyes.

"You're a fine fellow," she told him. Could she pull out her camera without alarming him? As if he knew what was in her mind he flew off.

She stood up and brushed down her jeans. What was Olivia doing at this moment? Was she packing her bags ready to go off tomorrow, expecting Nic to go with her? No doubt she was still seething about the latest argument with herself.

She had definitely made clear her opinion of Nic's PA more than once and now she had issued an ultimatum . . . leave or I'll broadcast my suspicions about you and Craig Hendon.

Whatever happened after this it would be open warfare between the two of them. Would Nic want that? It would hardly create the peaceful and friendly atmosphere he was taking pains to create for Trailover. He might well feel that for the sake of that she would have to go.

With a heavy heart, Melissa walked slowly across the grass. There was no sign of Olivia when she pushed open the back door and went through the empty kitchen and into the hall.

The office door stood open but there was no-one there. Poppy had left a cold lunch for them in the dining-room. There was no sign of her either which wasn't surprising. Melissa knew she had planned a visit to the supermarket in Swanford this afternoon.

Relieved to be on her own, Melissa ate quickly. She had picked up a leaflet, now replaced, from the reception desk in passing and read with interest what it said about the formation of the small museum in Trant Magna and the ease of making an appointment to view anything not at present on display.

A return visit would take care of the afternoon and get her out of Nic and Olivia's way. Great, no problems there. She would take every hour as it came and not to think too much of the future. Or the past.

She carried the plates and cutlery she had used into the kitchen and stacked them in the dishwater.

The front door bell rang. Melissa paused for a moment, and then went to answer it. Relax, she told herself. Damien was miles away.

Three young people stood outside wearing walking gear and with heavy rucksacks on their backs. The tallest of them shrugged his way out of his and dumped it on the ground. "Hi there," he said in a surprisingly deep voice. "We were told you had accommodation here for one night. A twin and a single."

His companions, both girls, took their rucksacks off too and looked at her expectantly.

Melissa indicated that they should enter. "Let's see what we have." She found the bookings register in the desk drawer and opened it. She knew there were vacant rooms on the top floor and it took moments only to sign them in. "You've come a long way," she said when she saw their Yorkshire addresses.

"We got a lift down from Leeds," said the younger of the two girls. "The chap ran us to the end of your drive."

Leeds? Melissa's heart missed a beat. With a determined effort she smiled at them.

"We've come to see the village," the other girl explained. "I'm doing a special study of abandoned villages as part of my course at college. Dad's treating us for tonight. You see, there's nowhere else within walking distance. I'm Sam. Rod and Millie came with me for moral support."

The other two grinned and Melissa saw the family likeness between them.

"Is the village far from here?" Rod asked.

Melissa glanced out of the window to check that the red flag had been lowered. "Lucky it's Friday afternoon," she said. "The village is usually open at weekends, and today they've opened the road early."

"Great," he said. "We've got to be on our way north early tomorrow so we've not much time. How do we get to the place?"

"I'll give you a lift down in my car if you like," Melissa said, surprising herself. For some reason they brought out a protective feeling in her even though they were only a year or two younger than she was. "It's a couple of miles away, an easy walk down there, a steep one back. You won't mind walking one way?"

"Hey, no," Rod said, smiling broadly. "Thanks."

She indicated the lift. "Let me show you to your rooms first."

Melissa was waiting in the hall when they came downstairs again. Their faces glowed with enthusiasm. They seemed as if nothing in life had yet touched them, and they had never known indifference, unfairness, betrayal. She hoped they hadn't.

They all piled into the car, Rod in the front passenger seat, the girls in the back. They looked even younger now they had shed their thick jackets. Millie's long dark hair was loose round her face.

Sam patted her fair hair as if she wasn't quite sure she liked her short style. Rod was silent as they drove down the narrow lane, looking about him with interest and not replying to the girls' chatter.

The car park was beginning to fill up as they arrived. Melissa parked by the boundary wall. "The village is over there," she told them. "You can just see one of the cottages through the bushes. I'll leave you to it, then. Enjoy yourselves. You saw on the information sheet that dinner is at seven-thirty?"

"See you," they chorused.

They loped off and she watched them go with a feeling of pleasure. She could imagine the Colonel and his ladies making a fuss of them when they got back to the hotel.

Melissa waited until they were out of sight and set off through the parked cars to the far entrance of the car park, heading for the track that led down to the beach. She pulled out her camera and slid the case off to stuff into the pocket of her jeans.

The light was good, and since she was here this was a good opportunity to take shots of one or two of the derelict tanks that had been left at the edge of the ranges.

She found herself glancing along the rows of cars, expecting any minute to see Damien's green Mondeo among them. But this was madness. He might well have changed his car by now. In any case why should he be down here in the village? Wouldn't he go straight to the hotel if he wanted to find her?

Her heart lurched as she saw a car very like his. A different registration number! She let out a gasp of relief. Stop it, she told herself, still breathing heavily. She was turning into a neurotic fool. At this rate Olivia would have a good case to fire her because she wouldn't be fit to concentrate on her work.

Deep in thought, Melissa left the car park behind her and walked down across the grass to join the track. A figure stood on the bridge that spanned the stream, the shadow from the surrounding bushes darkening his face. "Melissa!" he exclaimed.

"Nic!" Her voice came out with a squeak of surprise. "What are you doing here?"

The lines round his eyes deepened as he frowned. "I could ask you the same question."

Melissa hesitated. There was no reason at

all for her to feel on the defensive. Her feelings were caused by the shock of seeing him, she told herself. That, and the relief he wasn't Damien whom she had stupidly expected to be waiting for her.

She took a deep breath and clutched her camera to her closely. "I gave someone a lift down here," she said.

He raised one eyebrow. "Not from the hotel?"

She nodded. "They've booked in for one night."

"You shouldn't act as a taxi service," he said. "You're setting a precedent and that's not good."

She gazed back at him. She could feel his disapproval. Had Olivia filled him in on her assumptions about herself and Craig? Forget that rubbish, she told herself. She hastened to tell him about Rod and the girls and their enthusiasm not to waste a moment in visiting the village because they hadn't much time.

It all seemed so reasonable to her that she wondered he didn't see it too. But his frown was still there and when she finished she saw dark shadows beneath his eyes. "I'm off to take more photos," she said.

Nic stared broodingly at the stream, seeming intent on scrutinising the weed that floated at the edge where the water made indents into the sandy bank. "I've been walking," he murmured. "I need some time and space."

Melissa was silent, not knowing how to respond to his bitter-sounding words. She had a good idea of why he felt like this but could hardly say so. A surge of anger against Olivia rose in her that she could treat him the way she did.

He had enough to deal with without the added hassle of her demands to sell up here and move on. Why was she unable to understand his feelings for Trailover? They ran more deeply than a mere desire for money and success.

They were part of the man. Melissa moved her camera from one hand to the other. Nic had a lot to think about and now she was detaining him. She made a move to go.

"You're happy here?" he asked abruptly.

Surprised, she paused. "It's my sort of place," she said. She couldn't imagine, now, wanting to be anywhere else. She loved the smell of peat and damp earth, the bare landscape, the line of hillside stark against the sky, the scent of broom and the short springy turf of the cliff-tops.

"It's lonely here for you," he said.

"But beautiful."

He nodded. "Yes, beautiful." His eyes moved thoughtfully over her face.

In the ensuing silence she felt her heart thudding. She became aware that she was gripping her camera so tightly her fingers hurt. She took a deep calming breath. "I like the enthusiasm of our three new guests," she said quickly. "I want more people to love the place. I promise not to run a taxi service for them all."

"I'll hold you to that," he said with the flicker of a smile.

She smiled. "I've just had the most brilliant idea. Why don't I organise a weekly minibus trip to places of interest along the Jurassic coast? We'd be spoilt for choice."

She thought of people like Miss Fletching and her cousin who didn't like driving for long periods. There wouldn't always be the Colonel around to oblige. "The minibus could go farther afield and visit places guests might not find for themselves."

She had caught his interest now. He stood with one hand on the balustrade and gazed at her thoughtfully. "I'll do some sums and get on to a few coach companies for estimates," he said.

"I'll do that," Melissa said. "And I'll draw up a list of suitable places to visit and suss out places to eat and to have coffee breaks."

"Don't get in too deeply too quickly," he warned. "And keep it to yourself for the time being."

Did he mean he didn't want Olivia to know until the scheme was up and running? His eyes looked brighter now and he had lost his air of strain. She was glad her idea had done this for him.

"I'll be the soul of discretion," she said. "Just give me thirty minutes to take a few more photos and then I'll be back at the hotel scrutinising all those leaflets on display. I knew they were there for a reason!"

"During your time off?"

"Why not? I can't wait."

"Remember in your pricing that we'll need an information pack for everyone."

"I'll research it all and get one prepared," she said with confidence. "I'd like to do that. I'll try to make it interesting and informative." She knew her eyes shone with enthusiasm. She couldn't wait to make a start. The tourist office in Trant was close to the museum and she could visit both easily. She had the feeling that the Colonel's ladies would get a kick out of fossil hunting on Charmouth beach. "I'll get on to the Heritage Centre and find out what they've got to say," she added.

"Hey, wait a minute," he said. "You're

leaving me behind here."

She gave him a brilliant smile. "Not for long I hope."

The tourist office was helpful. She had the names of three coach companies, as well as advice on suitable locations and information about websites that should prove useful. The museum next, she thought.

She crossed the road, deep in thought. She knew the curator would be on hand to open the inner door because she had phoned from Trailover to arrange it. What she didn't expect was that she would bump into Craig at the entrance.

"Just coming to check up on something myself," he said, standing aside to let her go first.

She was glad he was there because he could say what else he would like her to catch with her camera. Together they followed the curator into the dim inner room. He flicked some light switches.

She saw there was a small shelf of objects that had come from the village, that was all. She clicked open her camera.

"A general shot I think, don't you?" Craig said. "Ah yes, here's the book I wanted to see again. It belonged to the schoolmaster of the time. I needed to check on the title."

They were soon finished and outside again.

"I was fascinated with the silver dwarfs in their velvet box I saw this morning," she said as they walked together down to the car park.

"Brilliant, aren't they? Some poor kid nicked them and then got sent away from the village in disgrace. Name of Joan Lambert, a foster child who'd only been there a few months."

"Joan Lambert?" Melissa said. She stopped and stared at him aghast. She had heard that name before. A memory stirred of herself and Nic in the library at the hotel soon after she had arrived. Sunshine had poured in through the tall windows and highlighted the rim of the desk in the middle of the room.

He was telling her about his grandmother. Joan Lambert? Yes, that was the name. A cold feeling trickled down her spine. Did Nic know this? She remembered the expression of affection on his face as he spoke of her living in the village as a young girl. It would be cruel to disillusion him. Expelled from the place as a common thief, oh dear.

"What's wrong?" Craig said, stopping too. Concern shone from his deep set eyes.

"How did you find that out?" she asked faintly.

He shrugged. "A piece of paper caught beneath the velvet lining in the box. It's still there I expect. The owner of the dwarfs seems to have been a tad vindictive. It's all there in a terse report. We'll never know the whole story. It was so long ago. Sad though."

As she drove down the lane to the hotel ten minutes later, Melissa couldn't get it out of her mind. There must have been some mistake surely? But Craig had seen the report in black and white. The little girl was only nine, an orphan by the sound of it, dumped with this Trailover family who perhaps hadn't wanted to take her in. It was a wonder her exercise book had survived and not burned in that old-fashioned tortoise stove that still stood in the corner.

But she was letting her imagination run away with her.

Nic had given no hint that there was anything untoward. In fact he seemed to be under the impression that his grandmother had lived there happily all her young life until the evacuation. It would be cruel to disillusion him.

But what of Craig's book? Wouldn't he want to include a juicy little story like this?

CHAPTER EIGHT

Much later, as she got ready for bed, Melissa thought over the events of her day. She was glad that she had decided to visit Trant again on her double mission, even though she had discovered something disturbing.

She felt choked with the knowledge she had gained, though it was as well that she had found this out now so she had the chance to do something about it.

If she could figure out what, of course. At the moment she had no idea. Should she ask Craig not to name Joan Lambert in his book without telling him the reason? How would he react to this piece of unwarranted interference on her part?

She didn't know him well enough to be sure but a man like Craig who had already done so much research was going to want to know more once his interest was aroused. Could she risk that?

Showered and in her towelling robe,

Melissa went to the window and pulled aside the curtains. Outside, the night was silent and the hills black against the darkening sky. She leaned on the windowsill, thinking hard.

If she told Nic what she had learned this afternoon he would be devastated that the whole concept of his being here was based on a lie. How could she tell him what had really happened? He might not believe her but he had only to contact Craig to find out the truth. To anyone else it might not matter because he was making a success of his hotel business here at Trailover. This would change nothing of that.

But Nic would be changed. He would know that his grandmother had lied and what would that do to him? His love for her memory would suffer. He would feel betrayed, and she knew only too well how betrayal felt.

She couldn't do this to him.

Melissa woke next morning, unrefreshed and no nearer deciding what she must do. At breakfast, the three youngest guests were absent, though she had noticed their bulging rucksacks placed ready in the hall.

"By heck, they'll have to get a move on if they want to eat," Poppy said when Melissa asked her where they were. "Gone off for a walk somewhere, I think. I'll have to clear at nine-thirty. The room's got to be ready for the meeting at ten."

For a moment Melissa had forgotten that Nic had booked in representatives of a firm from Southampton. They wanted to take a look at the place and discuss terms for a group of their clients for some sort of bonding session.

The dining-room had seemed the best place for this, especially as they wanted food laid on for a buffet lunch. "I'll go and look for Rod and the girls and round them up," she said as she drained her coffee.

There was no sign of them in the grounds or on the drive. Dew glistened on the yellow gorse flowering on the rough ground on the other side of the fence and the flagpole was empty. In the distance a seagull called. She walked to the top of the drive, seeing nobody.

Then she heard voices, faint in the distance. Surely it couldn't be the missing three? Alarmed, she gazed across the rugged ground and saw two figures on the skyline, immediately joined by another.

She waved frantically. They waved back, obviously unconcerned. She shouted, but there was no answer. They were too far inside the forbidden territory to hear her. She had to get them back before anything happened. Unexploded shells sometimes got left behind which was why it was dangerous to stray from the road or the designated footpaths. Her mouth felt dry.

Gingerly she climbed over the boundary fence and set off to reach them.

They greeted her with cheers.

"Come away," she gasped out. "This is forbidden ground. We'll be in deep trouble if anyone sees us."

"Shot at dawn?" Rod said with mock solemnity.

"Too good to miss being up here," Sam said. "What a glorious day. Look, you can see the deserted village from here."

"And the sea," Millie said, swinging back her long hair.

"You've got to come back at once," Melissa said desperately. "No-one's allowed to wander off the paths." She didn't want to alarm them by pointing out the dangers but it might come to that if she couldn't convince them.

Rod grinned at her. "We'll take you prisoner if you're not careful. Ransom you to the army. We'll demand a high price." They seemed in no mood to move.

"Don't joke," she implored. "This is serious."

"We'll come quietly if you take our photo first," Sam said.

"But only then," Rod said, putting out his hand for her camera. "I'll take you three girls against that odd bit of derelict machinery with the sea behind you."

"Be quick then," Melissa said. She would have to go along with it to get them away.

Seconds later they were leaping down the hillside. Melissa didn't breathe freely until they were back over the fence and into the safety of the drive.

"No harm done," Sam said, gasping a little as she smiled.

Melissa hung behind as they entered the hotel, her heart still beating faster than normal. Suppose she hadn't got them back and they had wandered farther into territory where they weren't supposed to be? Unexploded shells apart, the hotel would have been in deep trouble as they were guests. The phone lines would have been red-hot, headlines in the local paper and the name of Trailover House Hotel mud.

Rod and the girls ate a hasty breakfast and then hauled up their rucksacks preparing to leave. To Melissa's surprise Nic brought his car to the front door and got out to open the boot.

"Thanks for offering us a lift to Swanford," Sam said.

"A pleasure," Nic said, taking her rucksack from her.

Thank goodness Nic didn't know what they had been up to, Melissa thought.

Millie handed hers over too and turned to Melissa to give her a hug. "You're a mate," she said. "See you again one day."

"Make sure you're still here," Sam said, doing the same.

Melissa laughed as she released her. "Who knows?"

She caught Nic's glance for a moment as he placed Rod's rucksack with the others and slammed shut the boot lid. It was swift but penetrating and she wondered for a worrying moment if he knew about the trespass earlier. But no-one had seen her clamber over the fence to go in pursuit of the others, she was sure of it. If he had she would have heard about it by now.

The car drove off with all three passengers waving out of the windows. She was sorry to see them go. They had livened the place up for the short time they had been here though she could have done without the fright earlier.

Sighing, she went indoors. Olivia was

seated at the reception desk with the bookings register open before her. "A phone message for you," she said.

Melissa's heart twisted. "Yes?"

"He wants you to phone him as soon as you're free."

"Craig?"

"Craig." Olivia's voice was thick with suspicion. "I said you'd contact him as soon as you're off duty. Please don't make private calls in working hours. And it doesn't do to be too familiar with the guests either."

The injustice of it brought warm colour to Melissa's cheeks. She was prevented from answering by the phone ringing again.

Olivia snatched up the receiver. This time it was a booking enquiry. "I'll hand you over to my assistant now she's decided to come back," Olivia said dismissively as she got up.

Seething, Melissa settled in her place. She gave the information needed and noted down the name, address and telephone number. Olivia was really too much. Thank goodness she had gone upstairs.

The office would be clear for the moment and she would be able to get on to the coach company in peace.

She needed to make a provisional booking for a minibus for the following Wednesday, and then draw up an itinerary and get back to them again with her proposed route.

She moved into the inner office and set to work. After a while she heard Nic next door, moving about. Then he appeared in the connecting doorway looking slightly ruffled. Another problem?

"Is my engagement diary anywhere about?" he asked.

She saved her work and stood up. "Isn't it in your desk?"

"Someone's moved it."

Melissa had a good idea who that someone might be, but went into the main office to search. She found it on the top of the bookcase.

He looked at it with suspicion when she handed it to him.

"I thought so," he said, opening it and running his hand down the page.

"Impossible to get away next Friday for the weekend as I told Olivia. It's the day of the Lander Phillips clients' visit and they want to stay overnight. Could you talk to Poppy? I'd like a special dinner laid on for the three of them and some other important guests in my private apartment. Ten of us all told. Could you do that?"

"I'll do it now."

He smiled briefly. "Great, thanks. I'd like

a special effort made as it happens to be Olivia's birthday. D'you think Poppy can cope with that? We'll keep it a surprise for Olivia, I think. I'll leave it to you then, Melissa. Oh, and you're invited, too."

Melissa smiled though her heart sank. She was the last person Olivia would want at her party. In fact she wasn't sure Olivia would approve of the idea at all if she had set her heart on going off somewhere with Nic. And Poppy wouldn't be too enthusiastic, either.

"Why couldn't Nic ask me himself?" she demanded when Melissa found her in the laundry room.

Melissa smiled. "Take it easy, Poppy."

"Is he thinking I won't be able to cope and sent you to ask me instead?"

"Cope, you? You could cope with a whole army of them."

Poppy dumped the pile of clean towels she was holding on to the workbench. "We'll show him, and her."

"I'm sure you will," Mel said soothingly. "And I'll be glad if you count me in to help."

Poppy looked at her shrewdly. "Something on your mind?"

"Nothing I can't handle," Melissa said, hoping it was true. Having something like this to think about might calm her mind into making the right decision.

Somehow she must make Craig see the advisability of keeping Joan Lambert's name out of his book. Wasn't there something about libel even after a person's death if it affected their descendants? She would look into it on the Internet as soon as she had a spare moment.

Olivia was looking well on the night of the dinner party. Her dark hair, loose about her face, made her seem younger and more vulnerable. She smoothed her hands down the sides of her red dress as she smiled up at the tallest of the guests as they assembled on the terrace outside.

As she moved among the others, no-one would believe the fuss she had made earlier when she discovered Nic's plans for the evening. The calm atmosphere seemed almost too good to be true.

Nic introduced Melissa to everyone. They were polite to her, but she could see they weren't really interested in hearing how she was settling down at Trailover. Since they all appeared to be enjoying themselves she was content to stand to one side and listen to all the talk as she sipped her sherry.

Poppy had excelled herself with the preparations for the meal, and the guests all knew each other. The elements were all there for a successful evening. All the same she couldn't quite rid herself of the feeling that something was about to happen. Perhaps this merely stemmed from Olivia's bad grace at being denied the weekend away she had so craved.

Poppy, trim in dark skirt and white frilly blouse, shot Melissa a look of conspiracy as she announced that dinner was served. Olivia led the way through the open french windows.

Nic, standing aside with Melissa until the last, turned to her with a smile. "I think it's going well, don't you?"

She smiled, too, and agreed. He looked taller this evening in his tuxedo, more distinguished somehow. He was easily the most handsome man here. She almost felt shy of him as if he was a complete stranger.

He indicated that she should go before him. She had placed herself halfway down on the side of the table nearest the door so she could slip out easily to help Poppy if she was needed.

Poppy had chosen the menu well and her cooking was superb. Compliments flowed, and Poppy's face was flushed with pleasure as she collected the plates afterwards.

Melissa stood up to help her but was dissuaded by a frown from Nic. Poppy saw it, too, and gave Melissa a grin. The orange soufflé that followed was appreciated, too. Coffee afterwards was served in Nic's sitting-room.

Poppy carried in the coffee tray and placed it on the low table in front of Melissa. "Over to you," she said quietly.

"It's all been great," Melissa murmured. "Well done you!"

She was glad to have something to do. When she had provided them all with coffee as they liked it she relaxed in her seat to drink her own. She let the talk flow round her, pleased that the evening was going well and that Nic could show his friends what Trailover could do.

They were talking now about the proposed day tours of the Jurassic coast and Melissa's part in suggesting them. Stop, she wanted to warn Nic as he began to heap praise on her.

This was not the right time for that. Olivia's frown of displeasure should have told him that this was a forbidden subject. And on her birthday, too. Melissa almost felt sorry for her.

At last Olivia could stand it no longer. "Ah yes," she drawled. "Melissa, the perfect

PA. Efficient as they come. Clean as a whistle, too, apart from her clandestine affair with a married man."

For a give-away second Nic's eyes flashed. Melissa tried hard to keep her face expressionless. Poppy, appearing in the doorway in the moment of deep silence that followed, looked as if she would drop the pot of fresh coffee she was carrying.

She took a deep breath and with great care placed it on the table. She straightened, her face pinched with disapproval, and then stumped off.

As she did so a burst of talk started. No-one, it seemed, wished to comment on what they had just heard. Nic leaned back in his chair, his eyes half-closed. Melissa had seen enough of Olivia's expression to know she had intended her remark to do harm.

She felt stunned and deeply hurt, unable to frame the words of denial. Thankful that no-one spoke to her, she sank back in her chair and looked down at her hands in her lap.

She was glad when the evening ended at last in a flurry of goodbyes. There was the crunch of gravel as the guests drove away.

"A perfect evening, thanks to you and Poppy, Melissa," Nic said as he closed the front door behind them and put his arm

116

round Olivia.

The kitchen door burst open. "I'll not stay here and see injustice done," Poppy cried.

"Injustice?" Nic said. "What's up, Poppy? I was just coming to congratulate you on a first-class meal."

Poppy almost spat in indignation. "Fair's fair and that accusation wasn't fair. Either Olivia goes or I do."

Appalled, Melissa stared at her. No prizes for guessing who would be expected to leave Trailover if it came to the point.

Poppy seemed in no doubt about that either. "I'm off upstairs to pack," she said as she slammed shut the door and stormed off.

Before she reached the first landing Melissa was after her. "Please, Poppy, stop," she cried as she ran.

But Poppy was having none of it. Melissa was gasping for breath as she raced after her to the second floor and along the passage that led to her room. She was too late and Poppy's door slammed in her face. She heard the key turn in the lock and the sounds of cupboard doors opening and shutting.

"Come on, Poppy, we need to talk." Melissa breathed deeply, willing her to turn the key. It warmed her to know that she had a champion in Poppy but not that she had reacted so strongly in her defence that she would do herself harm by rushing off when she had nowhere to go.

What had got into her to make her react like this? They had laughed together about Olivia's nasty remarks often enough.

To her relief Poppy opened the door but her flushed face and staring eyes alarmed Melissa. "Please, Poppy, calm down," she said as she went in and saw the untidy mess of an upturned drawer on Poppy's bed.

"How can I when that woman insults you in front of all those people?"

"Get it in perspective, Poppy. We ignore Olivia like always. Right? What do those people care about it, anyway? No-one's going to take any notice of a throw-away remark like that."

"Except Nic," Poppy said.

"But I don't care what Nic's opinion is of me," Melissa said. She thought of him leaning back in his chair, his eyes half-closed. She had no idea of what he had been thinking especially when she hadn't denied it. But of course he would believe Olivia.

It was a wonder he hadn't already demanded to know what she was doing on Friday night when she should have been on duty in the hotel. As of course she was.

Poppy stomped across to the other side of the bed. "She shouldn't be allowed to get away with it."

"I'll confront her myself in the morning."

"A fat lot of good that will do."

Melissa knew she was right. "It's too late to leave tonight, Poppy," she said in desperation.

Poppy almost spat in her indignation. "I'll not change my mind." She opened a drawer in the bedside table and routed about furiously.

Melissa sank down on the bed and watched her for a moment, thinking hard. She had to do something to make her see sense but Poppy was in no mood for argument.

"Let's both sleep on it," she said wearily. "If you still want to go, I'll help you pack in the morning."

Poppy stopped what she was doing and looked at her intently. "Don't deny that woman got to you."

Melissa stared down at her hands. Of course she had been upset and alarmed when Olivia came out with that stupid remark that she must have known was untrue. But Nic didn't. She bit her lip, reliving the moment again and wishing she had made some retort at the time.

CHAPTER NINE

Melissa heard Poppy moving about soon after six next morning. She leapt out of bed at once to wash and dress, her mind on the problem ahead. Trying to talk Poppy out of something she had made up her mind to do wouldn't be easy, but she would have a thumping good try. A different approach perhaps, something more subtle.

She was down in the kitchen first and had pulled open the curtains to reveal the fresh, sunny morning outside before Poppy came in. She was dressed in a blouse and skirt and had her meagre hair pulled back from a face that looked white and pinched.

"I could do with a cup of tea," she said as she slumped down on a stool. "Right good and strong."

Melissa set about making one in silence. She would let Poppy speak first. All her own arguments had been useless last night and probably wouldn't be much better this morning.

"What should I do without you?" Poppy said as she watched Melissa pour tea into her mug.

"You'll soon be finding out," Melissa said as she sat down at the table opposite her. "You've checked the times of the coach from Swanford?"

Poppy took the mug that Melissa passed to her. "What sort of remark's that?"

Good. She sounded uncertain. Melissa took a deep breath. "Teach me what you do as a housekeeper," she said as she raised her mug of tea to her lips and then put it down again. "How you choose menus, what lists you make. All that. I'll learn to cook. I'll stand in for you, Poppy. I expect it's quite easy."

Poppy stared in astonishment. "You? But you can't do two jobs."

"Try me."

"No way. I'll not have that."

Melissa tried not to smile. "Then what's to be done?"

"Get someone else in, of course."

"Oh, come on, Poppy. That's not easy at the last minute. You know it isn't. What will Miss Fletching and Mrs Bond do if they can't rely on you for a friendly chat and a cup of tea when they come back in from their jaunts? Colonel Beale likes your cooking and his poor wife will fade away without sustenance when she gets out of hospital in a couple of days. You know they've booked for a further fortnight so she can convalesce? Please, Poppy, think again. It won't do me much good to be here without you either, will it?"

"You've got an easy tongue on you."

"And you've got an easy way of treating the guests as if they're your friends. They appreciate it, Poppy. We all do."

"We all do what?" Nic said, pushing open the door.

Melissa looked round in dismay. How long had Nic been outside listening in? He wasn't usually up this early. "We appreciate everything Poppy does at Trailover," she said quietly.

He inclined his head in agreement, looking at Poppy. "I think we need to talk," he said. "Finish your tea, Poppy, and join me in my dining room."

"I've yet to clear in there," Poppy said dismissively.

"The office then."

"D'you think I'm getting the push?" Poppy said as she finished drinking her tea and scraped back her stool to stand up.

She sounded as if she minded and Melissa

smiled. "I very much doubt it, Poppy," she said. "You're far too valuable here."

Her relief might be short-lived though, she reminded herself as she made her way to Nic's dining-room. It was still early and she needed something to keep her occupied while this was all being sorted out.

She lifted the arrangement of silk roses from the centre of the table and placed it carefully on the side table by the window. As she started to collect the table mats together, the door opened and Olivia came in.

"What do you think you're doing in Nic's private apartment?" she demanded.

She was the last person Melissa wanted to see, especially in the belligerent mood she seemed to be in so often these days. She picked up the mats and held them close to her.

Olivia, in her black jeans and sweatshirt, looked like a bad fairy. And that's just what she was, Melissa thought as she moved towards the drawer where the mats were kept, a bad spirit in the place. What bad spell was she planning to cast this bright morning?

"That won't be necessary," Olivia said coldly. "Leave them on the trolley. I'll deal with them myself."

Melissa did as she said. It was all the same to her where the mats went. She picked up some spare cutlery and placed it on a tray ready to be taken to the kitchen.

"I shall be getting the table laid for two," Olivia went on. "We're eating early, Nic and myself, before we leave."

"Leave?"

"Yes, leave. Nic is driving me up to London and we plan to get away as soon as we can. You don't think we want to stay here after last night's fiasco, do you?"

Melissa looked at her in silence. Was she referring to her accusation or did she mean Poppy's threats to leave them in the lurch? Obviously the latter. Olivia wouldn't have liked Poppy's ultimatum even when she was sure of her position. "How long will you be away?" she asked.

Olivia shrugged. "As long as it takes. Nic will be driving straight back, of course. He can't afford to be away from the place in the circumstances. There are certain things he needs to look into.

"His suspicions about that man, Craig Hendon, for a start. He's going to insist he sees that book he's writing before it goes off to a publisher. He doesn't trust him an inch, or you either. Now you two are collaborating in more ways than one, anything could happen. No-one likes being made a fool of. We fear misconceptions and falsities that will show Nic up as a fraud."

Melissa felt the colour drain from her face. "That's not true."

"No? Can you prove it?" Olivia said triumphantly.

She looked so smug standing there in her witch-like attire that Melissa wanted to push her roughly out of the room. "I believe Nic trusts me to do my best for Trailover."

Olivia smiled but her eyes were cold. "And that included spending the night before last elsewhere, when you should have been on duty here? You were seen returning in the early morning. You can't deny it."

"I most certainly can," Melissa said, holding angry words back with difficulty. She could stand it no longer. She picked up the tray. "I'll be in the kitchen if Nic needs me," she said, her voice tight.

She was seething by the time she had placed the tray on the draining board and opened the dishwasher to unload it. She lifted out the cutlery container and banged it down on the worktop with a clatter. That woman!

It was on Saturday morning that Rod and the girls had gone wandering off on to the ranges and she had followed them to bring them back from what might have been a dangerous situation.

She had the photo Sam had taken to prove it. The direction of the shadows showed that the photo had been taken in the early morning. Rod stood there on the hillside with his arms round herself and Millie. They were all grinning happily as they posed by the derelict building.

No-one could doubt where they were . . . on the ranges where they shouldn't have been and looking happy about it. Proof enough that she hadn't been with Craig.

She looked up in surprise at the sound of gravel crunching outside and a car moving off. Rushing to the window, she was in time to see Nic's car disappear up the drive. So, they were off already. Nic hadn't seen fit to find her to tell her his plans and that hurt. His suspicions of her obviously ran deep.

"Are you coming with us, dear?" Mrs Bond asked as she and her cousin came up to the reception desk where Melissa was seated after breakfast.

She looked up at her in surprise and then remembered that today was the first of the planned outings to the Jurassic coast. She had booked the minibus for ten o'clock. How could she have forgotten?

She smiled. "Not this time, I'm afraid. Nic

has had to be away and I'm on duty in his place."

"No trouble, I hope?"

"Oh, no," Melissa said, doing her best to sound confident. Thankfully, last night's crisis had been sorted out and Poppy had agreed to stay, but not before telling Nic exactly what she thought of Olivia's false accusations.

"Perhaps next time?"

Melissa smiled. "You've got all the leaflets and information?"

"Oh, yes, dear."

"Be sure to bring me back a fossil," she said in mock earnest.

This was the first of these day trips she had arranged and a bit of an experiment. They were to visit one or two places before lunch and then afterwards someone was going to meet the party at the Bidmouth Heritage Centre and give an introductory talk.

Then their party would set off for the fossil walk along the beach in the hope of finding some for themselves. It should be a good day out, even without a guide for the whole of the day.

Time seemed to stretch endlessly in front of Melissa as the minibus set off. It was Poppy's day for shopping in Swanford so

Melissa had the place to herself. Filling in the notes for the day in the day-to-day diary took less than twenty minutes. She replaced it in the desk in the main office and then looked round for something to occupy her.

The records of bookings were all up to date and the menus prepared and typed out for the coming week. On the back of the chair Nic had left his navy sweatshirt. She straightened it, smoothing the material, overwhelmed with the longing to be with him now wherever he was on the road to London.

She had told Poppy that it was no consequence to her what Nic thought of her, but she knew it wasn't true. He had said nothing last night about the accusation Olivia had made against her and she had had no opportunity to defend herself.

She picked up the sweatshirt and held it to her face breathing in the masculine smell of him. It was almost too much to bear that he probably believed Olivia's lies. Even now, in the car beside him, she might be elaborating on her accusation, discussing with him what they should do about it.

Melissa sighed and replaced the garment, knowing the long day ahead would be difficult to get through in her present unsettled state. She was doing no good lingering here.

Maybe she'd go upstairs to her room and finish the notes she'd started about the Trailover artefacts in the museum.

She jumped as the phone rang.

"Melissa."

"Hi, there, Nic," she said. His voice seemed close in the quiet office. In the background she heard soft music and the clatter of china. She imagined him seated in some luxury hotel surrounded by rich furnishings. Crimson wall-hangings perhaps and the scent of freshly-brewed coffee. Olivia, seated beside him, would look bored and impatient as he switched on his mobile. But would he have it switched on in a place like that?

"I have an apology to make, he said. "A last-minute conference-type meeting booked in for tomorrow and I forgot to tell you. More relaxed than the last one and they'd like to wander about outside if the weather's good and perhaps hold the sessions on the terrace. That's why I'm coming back tonight as I want to take part."

"Ah," Melissa said, letting her breath out slowly. "Lunch as last time?"

"A buffet lunch outside perhaps. Could you warn Poppy? You'll see to all the arrangements your end?"

"Of course," she said, her spirits lifting.

So Olivia had got it wrong and the reason for Nic's swift return had nothing to do with not trusting her? A warm feeling stole round her heart. Olivia got a lot of things wrong.

"And thanks," he said. I'll see you later. Oh, and Melissa, did you get the message about the phone call?"

"Phone call?"

"A friend of yours. Just as we were leaving. Something about calling in on you later today. I left a message on the reception desk. Feel free to entertain anyone you choose."

Was it her imagination or had a certain coldness crept into Nic's voice?

"Thank you," she said faintly and put the phone down.

There was no message on the desk. Melissa moved the piles of leaflets from one side to the other. Then she checked the floor in case the note had dropped off. Nothing. In any case she knew whom to expect. It as coming at last, the visit she had been dreading from Damien. So what? He couldn't hurt her now.

Concentrate on the arrangements for the conference tomorrow, she told herself as she carefully replaced everything as she had found it. Nic hadn't said how many would be attending, and in her relief that this was the reason for his swift return, she had forgotten to ask. Never mind, Poppy would prepare plenty of food for all and anything not used would be frozen for their own use at some later date. No problem there.

Melissa went along to the conference room and checked that the seating was arranged in two rows in a wide informal semicircle in case it was needed. The long low table by the window was suitable on which to serve coffee if the weather was poor and there were easy chairs nearby to give the room a relaxed atmosphere. Since Olivia was away, some flower arrangements would be good too.

She heard a car approaching as she went out to the front drive to cut some ivy from the fence. This was it, then? In spite of herself, her heart flipped. The last time she had seen Damien, he had come straight from someone else's arms and that painful memory rose to the surface now.

Bracing herself, she looked up. A blue car, very like her own, came crunching down across the gravel. Leonie? The blood seemed to leave Melissa's body and then come rushing back. Leonie, here? She stared in wonder as the car drew level with her and stopped.

CHAPTER TEN

Leonie looked pale, her dark hair lank. She was wearing a yellow shirt and the metal medallion on a black thong round her neck looked totally wrong. "I had to come," she gasped as if the words were wrung out of her.

Still staring, Melissa nodded.

"Don't send me away, Mel, please. We need to talk."

Again Melissa nodded. "Pull in down there near the house," she said. "I'll follow you."

She could see, when Leonie got out, that she had lost a lot of weight. With a wave of her hand Melissa indicated that they should walk round to the sunny terrace on the other side of the house. "I'll make coffee," she said.

She was back as quickly as she could, hardly allowing herself to think. Leonie had seated herself where she could look across at the ranges. She accepted a mug of coffee and her hands trembled as she placed it on the low table nearby.

"I phoned," she said tentatively. "They said I should come. I wanted to see if you were all right."

"Is Damien with you?" Melissa asked, relieved that she could now say his name without pain.

Leonie shuddered and shook her head. "No way."

"Where is he, d'you know?"

"He went off. I don't know where. It was all wrong. I didn't mean . . . It just happened, Mel . . ." Leonie broke off and looked at her beseechingly.

Melissa raised one eyebrow and immediately thought of Nic and the way his eyebrows seemed to shoot up of their own volition. "You did me a good turn," she said.

Leonie leaned forward. "He wasn't right for you, Mel, or me either, but I didn't think you'd ever be grateful."

"Certainly not for the way it happened," Melissa said, feeling her face flame at the memory. "How could you, Leonie? A real mean trick. To lose a fiancé and a best friend . . ."

"I don't want you to lose a best friend," Leonie said miserably.

Melissa leapt up and went to the low wall that bounded the terrace on one side. She leaned on it, trembling. "I wanted to boil you in oil."

"I know. I'm sorry. And now?"

"Now?" Melissa swung round, her anger gone as quickly as it had come. "Now . . . I don't know. It's been a shock seeing you. I need time, that's all."

"I'll go," Leonie said humbly. "I'm on holiday in Bournemouth with my sister and her friend. I wanted to see you when I found out where you were."

Melissa looked at her closely. "How did you find out?"

"I made Damien tell me."

"He knew?"

Leonie nodded, still looking miserable. "He phoned this place on the off-chance before you arrived and spoke to the proprietor. He said you were expected and to phone back later."

Melissa was silent, thinking of the implications. From the beginning Nic had known that Damien was trying to contact her and had encouraged him. He had kept his own counsel, no doubt believing it was what she wanted. She looked at Leonie sitting hunched in her chair wearing that ridiculous medallion. Coming here had taken courage.

"Come back tomorrow," she said. "I'll feel better about it then."

They got up and stood facing each other. She would have time to think, to accept that what had happened was truly in the past and had helped to make her stronger, able to cope with what life threw at her. Already a load seemed to have dropped from her, leaving behind such peace she felt bathed in light.

Nic returned in the late afternoon just after the minibus pulled outside the front door. Melissa was aware that he looked tired but there was no time to greet him before going forward to meet the disembarking guests. Their outing had been as successful as she hoped and, smiling, Melissa turned to share this with Nic but he had gone.

He reappeared when they had dispersed and she saw that he had changed from his dark suit to light jeans and shirt. The strain about his eyes was still there.

"A word, please, Melissa," he said shortly.

She followed him to the office, her heart heavy.

He looked at her for a moment in silence before indicating that she should sit on the chair he pulled out for her. He seated himself on the opposite side and sat with his arms on the desk and his long fingers intertwined.

"Olivia feels concerned about your friendship with Craig Hendon," he said, looking at her closely. "No, don't interrupt until I've had my say. Your private life is your own concern, Melissa, except when it impinges on the good name of this place. You must understand that."

"I have no private life," she said.

He raised one eyebrow.

Aware that she sounded pathetic, Melissa tried to elaborate. "I mean not in the way you think. Craig has asked me to do the photographs for his book, that's all."

He unlaced his fingers. "I see."

Melissa's mouth felt dry. What did he see? That she was sitting here trying to do a cover-up? She clenched her hands in her lap, reminding herself that Nic had made it clear he would welcome any friend of hers to Trailover, and because of that Leonie had come. She mustn't forget his kindness in saying that.

"I wouldn't lie to you, Nic," she said quietly. This was an intolerable situation. She could prove the truth by producing the photograph Sam had taken in the early morning in question and that would prove she wasn't where Olivia had said she was.

But it would also prove something else,

far more potentially damaging to Trailover, that she had trespassed on the ranges in a dangerous area. Nic would be livid that she had disobeyed his orders. She would leave things as they were and let him think what he liked.

He pushed his chair back and stood up. "Then there's nothing more to be said."

She stood up too and met his eyes with a challenging look in her own. "May I go now?"

He inclined his head. Melissa left with as much dignity as she could but she was trembling as she went upstairs to tidy herself for the evening meal. So much had happened today she felt unable to think things through properly. She hadn't eaten much either. By the time she reached her room on the top floor she felt dizzy.

She let Olivia get the better of her, however hard she tried. She would stay here and prove her strength. And Leonie would be returning tomorrow. The thought of that was more heartening than she could have imagined.

By ten o'clock next morning the delegates had assembled for the conference and proceedings had begun on the terrace as planned. Leonie had phoned again and they had arranged for her to arrive this afternoon when people were leaving and Melissa would have time to talk.

All was in order and Melissa had time to relax. Immediately she sought out Poppy who was in the kitchen supervising the preparations for the buffet lunch.

"Need any help?" Melissa asked.

Poppy rinsed her hands at the sink and indicated, with a nod of her head, that everything was under control. "See you outside on the back terrace where we can hide away for a bit. I'll bring us a drink."

As they sat in the shade at the back of the house sipping homemade lemonade, Melissa felt more relaxed than she had for weeks. True there seemed to be something bothering Nic but it was probably nothing more than Olivia's absence.

"This is the life," Poppy said, placing her empty glass on the tray on the stone table.

The companionable silence between them was suddenly broken.

"Someone else has come," Poppy said sitting bolt upright.

Melissa put down her glass. She could hear voices. "Nic's dealing with it," she said.

The door from the staff dining-room opened and Poppy sprang up. "I'm off," she said in alarm. "I can't be caught out here." She escaped into the garden.

In the doorway stood Damien in dark jeans and red shirt.

"May I join you?" he said, coming forward. "Your boss assured me I'd be welcome."

Melissa placed her empty glass on the tray. "Then he's wrong," she said coldly. "We've nothing to say to each other Damien. I think you know that too." She marvelled that his presence failed to move her in any way. He could have been a mere acquaintance and not the man she had planned to spend the rest of her life with. She seemed to be another person too, completely sure of herself as she sat looking at him so calmly.

He moved towards her. "Aren't you going to invite me to sit down?"

"I don't think so."

"But Melissa . . ."

What could she say to get rid of him? "Please go, Damien. I wish you well in whatever you decide to do with your life, but please understand once and for all that it has nothing to do with me." She stood up to emphasise her words.

He stepped towards her and gripped her wrists. "I'm not going to accept that."

She flushed. "Let me go!"

"Not until you see sense."

"Let me go!" she cried again. Straining to

break free, she lost her balance and fell back against the table. The tray slithered off and crashed to the ground.

"Problems?"

She had never been so glad to see Nic. She struggled upright as Damien released her. "He's just going," she gasped.

Nic glared at Damien, every line of his body proclaiming his intention of ejecting him by force if necessary. "Get out!"

Damien looked about to argue but then changed his mind. He glowered at Melissa and left.

Still shocked at the suddenness of Damien's attack, Melissa clutched the table for support finding its solid immobility comforting. At once Nic sprang forward, his arms round her. She leaned thankfully against him. Damien's reaction had shocked her more than she would admit. But it was over. She took a deep shuddering breath.

"A friend of yours?" Nic said.

"Not any more," she said faintly.

He released her and pulled out a chair. "Here, sit down."

She looked helplessly at the shattered glass. "I'd better clear this up."

"Later. Poppy can organise someone to do it. Stay here. I'll check he's left the premises."

Melissa leaned back in her chair and closed her eyes. It was finally finished with Damien and her relief was enormous. Had she ever cared for him? It was difficult to imagine. Now all she felt was gratitude that he had gone and would bother her no more.

Nic was back within minutes carrying another tray of glasses. Instead of lemonade he had brought brandy. He poured some into the glasses. "Drink this," he commanded, handing one to Melissa.

She was glad to do as he told her and took several restorative sips.

"Good, the colour's back in your cheeks now," he said as she finished and put her glass down. "D'you want to tell me about it?"

She looked about her at the shady patio. Suddenly it seemed cold without the sun. "There's nothing to tell really," she said. "It was all finished before I arrived. You know we were to have married. He found . . . someone else. It didn't work out. But he found out where I was . . ."

Nic leaned forward. "My fault, I'm afraid. He phoned to check if you'd arrived. Naturally I assumed it was all in order." He raised the bottle. "Another?" his voice sounded lighter then and in his eyes she saw a wondering expression that made her heart tremble.

She dare not think what it might mean. She shook her head. "No, really." She felt stronger now but Damien's reaction had been a shock and she couldn't cope with anything more.

"It's a pity we can't get away from here for a short while," Nic said quietly. "It would do you the world of good to have a walk down to the beach."

"With the red flags flying?"

He leaned back and smiled ruefully. "That, of course. Not to mention having to be on the spot for our conference guests. You see how it is?"

She smiled too. "This is how you like it."

The expression in his eyes softened. "It's my life."

"I know that, Nic."

"Yes, I think you do. And what of you, Melissa? What of your life now that man is out of it?"

An impossible question to answer and she didn't try. Instead she picked up her glass and drank the last of her brandy. Then, gazing thoughtfully at her empty glass, she said, "I'm happy here."

"I had to phone Craig Hendon soon after the dinner party," Nic said.

"You did?"

He looked at her closely. "He wasn't there. His secretary said he was away on a week's leave."

For a moment the implications failed to sink in. Then she realised that here was proof that Olivia's accusations were false.

Nic moved slightly in his chair. "You don't seem relieved that the truth is out," he said.

"The truth was always out as far as I was concerned," she said.

"I couldn't believe you would lie."

"And you thought Olivia could?" she dared ask.

He got up abruptly and moved to the fence that separated the patio from the kitchen garden. Leaning on it, with his back to her, he was silent for some moments. His soft hair was slightly rumpled and she longed to stroke it flat. She saw that his cream silk shirt had a small flaw near the collar and that the light colour emphasised his tanned neck.

"Olivia won't be coming back," he said at last.

Surprised, Melissa could only stare. Was this a sudden decision? What did it mean? There seemed to be a connection here between his bald statement and her remark.

"She found a notebook of yours," he continued in an even voice. "Some research you'd been doing at the museum. She refused to give it back to you after she'd shown it to me. Evidence, she said. She wanted you out of here, Melissa."

"I didn't know it had gone missing," Melissa said. The notebook had been in her top drawer, safe she had thought. She hadn't checked on it lately. So the accusations Olivia had made about her planning to show Nic's enterprise up as a fraud had been based on true facts . . . her notes about his grandmother's disastrous six months with a Trailover family who didn't want her because she had been shown up as a common thief.

"There is no way I would have let Craig name her," she said.

"I believe you."

Melissa smiled. To hear that was sweet.

"We all make mistakes," Nic said gently as he turned round to face her. "Most of us have the opportunity to learn from them if we only take it. I think my grandmother did. I loved her very much. Nothing makes any difference to that."

Moved beyond words, Melissa looked down at her hands in her lap. "I haven't had a chance to talk to Craig yet," she said. "I promise it'll be all right. No one knows the reason behind what she did. No one knows her story. She was a little lost child . . ." she broke off, her lips trembling.

At once Nic leaned forward and took her hands. "As you were when you came here looking so brave in your bright clothes, but with a haunted look in these lovely eyes of yours. You had been betrayed too in a different way."

"Like everyone in the village of Trailover," she murmured. "Most of them dead now, like your grandmother."

"But not forgotten."

"Not forgotten," she agreed.

"And some good comes out of it, in the end. Think of our elderly guests full of appreciation for this part of the world. My grandmother made that possible, through me. And now there's you, my dear, Melissa. You have taught me that goodness and kindness are beautiful things and of far more value than material things."

"And trust," she said. "What of trust, Nic?"

He smiled. "That too."

She released her hands and pulled her camera from her pocket. Seconds later she found the shot she wanted on the viewing screen. "Look Nic," she said quietly. "Can you see where we are?"

He gazed at it for a long moment and she

was almost afraid to breathe. "They trespassed on the ranges the morning they left and you went after them?"

"I had to," she said simply. "I didn't want you or Trailover House to be in trouble if anyone saw them."

"So foolish but so brave," he murmured. "Had I known, I would have been terrified for your safety, loving you as I do."

She looked into the depths of his brown eyes in wonder, seeing there all she could hope for.

He pulled her close. "My beautiful one," he murmured into her hair.

She trembled in his arms. His lips, when they found hers, were warm. She relinquished all sense of time, secure in the knowledge at last she had come home.

We hope you have enjoyed this Large Print book. Other Thorndike, Wheeler, and Chivers Press Large Print books are available at your library or directly from the publishers.

For information about current and upcoming titles, please call or write, without obligation, to:

Publisher
Thorndike Press
295 Kennedy Memorial Drive
Waterville, ME 04901
Tel. (800) 223-1244

or visit our Web site at:

http://gale.cengage.com/thorndike

OR

Chivers Large Print
published by BBC Audiobooks Ltd
St James House, The Square
Lower Bristol Road
Bath BA2 3SB
England
Tel. +44(0) 800 136919
email: bbcaudiobooks@bbc.co.uk
www.bbcaudiobooks.co.uk

All our Large Print titles are designed for easy reading, and all our books are made to last.